THEN AND THERE, HERE AND WHERE

THEN AND THERE, HERE AND WHERE

Orabella the Oracle 1

ESABELLA STRICKLAND
MICHAEL STRICKLAND

Supervising Editors: Caitlin Chrismon
Associate Editor(s): Gabriella Gerace, Cameron Sessinger
Internal Formatting: Alexandria Boykin
Cover Designer: L. Austen Johnson
Cover Illustrator: Fariza Dzatalin

GenZPublishing.org
Aberdeen, NJ

Esabella: I dedicate this book to my hardworking mom, Kate, and of course, to my dad, who helped me write this story.

Michael: Without the love of Esabella, this book would not have been possible. To my mom, Emma, and my sister Janet in heaven. You're not forgotten.

To Meeko, our 16-year family cat. Meeko cooed like a bird and comforted us like a dog. He would wink when you said "I love you" to him, and he would put his paw on your arm to cheer you up. Meeko was more than a cat; he was our friend.

AUTHOR'S NOTE

This is a work of fiction. Although its form is that of memory, it is not one. Space and time have rearranged to suit the convenience of the book, and except for public figures, any resemblance to persons living or dead is coincidental. The opinions expressed are those of the characters and should not be confused with that of the authors.

PROLOGUE

"Mom, OH MY GOD! You did an amazing job on the costume!" I exclaimed as I flapped my arms like a raven, marvelling at all the black feathers she had sewn into my bodysuit. I walked out of my bedroom into the hallway where my mom stood waiting for me.

"Orabella, I still can't believe you wanted to go as Morrigan! She seems so dark," my mom said, walking over to me to adjust the headdress I had tightly secured into my caramel brown hair.

"Mom, I already told you: Morrigan is the Celtic goddess of birth and death, she's perfect for the Summer Solstice Festival!" I pushed away from her to whip my head around, testing the security of the feathers.

"Well, you do look good with all those feathers," my mom said, backing away from my wild movements.

Satisfied that my headdress was still in place, I thought aloud, "I hope I don't get too hot in my costume, because I love it!"

"I think it's more suited for Halloween than this community event," my mom said, eyeing my dark face paint and black lipstick.

"Nah! It's not scary enough!" I laughed.

"I suppose . . ." Mom said, a little bit skeptically.

"So, are you dressed up like a Greek warrior?" I asked, taking in her sandals, the toga-like dress, and her long brown hair pulled back in a strappy headband.

"I am going as Artemis, goddess of light."

"Cool! You're such a baddie, Mom," I gushed. Mom's cheeks turned a deep shade of red at the compliment.

"Well, as you know, the summer solstice was originally a celebration of light's triumph over darkness and of the bountiful beauty that light brings into our lives. So, now we get to celebrate the longest day of the year every year!"

Suddenly, Dad walked out of the bathroom into the hallway dressed in a long tunic, a furry cape, and a blonde beard that was pasted to his face haphazardly. I almost laughed out loud at him.

"Dad, you can't go to the community centre like that," I exclaimed, wondering what my friends would think when they saw him.

My mom laughed as my dad made some weird poses with his shield. I wanted to look away, but I couldn't take my eyes off of the silliness.

"Bella, I am going as the all-powerful Dutch god, Wodan," Dad said proudly.

"OH MY GOD, you have got to be kidding! Mom, tell him he can't go like that! I won't be able to go to school tomorrow, seriously," I demanded.

Mom giggled. "Bella, all the other parents will be dressed up too!"

"I don't care, Mom. He looks like a bad version of a Viking. Where did you even get that beard?" I asked my dad incredulously.

Ignoring my question, Dad said, "Don't be so self-conscious! It will be lots of fun! We'll get to learn all about how different cultures celebrate the solstice." He walked down the stairs to the front door with no motion to make any changes to his wardrobe.

"Oh God. Okay, let's go and get this over with," I said as I rolled my eyes.

It was only a short walk to the community centre from our house, but I hoped we were going to drive. I wanted to keep the noble Wodan hidden for as long as possible. Of course, we walked right past our car in the driveway and onto the sidewalk towards the community centre. I stayed as far in front of my parents as I could to minimize the chances of anyone recognizing my dad in his ridiculous costume, but since my dad was so tall, it was pretty useless trying to hide him from anyone we knew. As we got closer to the centre, I picked up my pace even more, as I knew I would be seeing my friends soon.

I looked down at my phone to text Alexa:

Where are you? I sent.

I am here with Olivia, we are waiting by the bathroom, Alexa responded.

Okay, I will be there in a few! Don't take off! I replied.

I turned around and shouted to Mom and Dad, "Heading in to meet up with Alexa and Olivia! I will see you later!"

Before they could respond, I took off and headed into the crowd.

The community centre was filled with lots of weird and cool costumes—now I wasn't feeling so awkward about my dad's appearance. I looked around for Alexa and Olivia, and when I finally spotted them, I ran towards them excitedly.

"Cool costume, Bella! Who are you supposed to be?" Alexa said as she touched the feathers running along the arms of my bodysuit.

"I'm Morrigan, goddess of life and death," I answered proudly, but then my voice dropped a little as I took in Olivia's costume. "Ah, Olivia . . . why do you look like a banana?"

"I told you!" Alexa responded, shooting a knowing glance at Olivia.

"Seriously? You guys have no imagination! I'm a crescent moon," Olivia snapped, a little defensively.

"Sorry, I didn't mean it like that! You look cool and bright," I said, trying to make up for making her feel self-conscious.

Then I turned to Alexa. "Where's your costume?" I asked.

"I'm just not into it," Alexa responded.

"Well, that's okay." I shrugged my shoulders and decided to change the subject. "Where are Scarlett and Lilou?"

"They're not coming. They don't think it's cool," Olivia said.

"Not cool? This is awesome! It's like Halloween during the summer," I protested.

"Oh well, let's get inside and see who else is here from school," Olivia suggested.

I then thought, I hope Rachelle and her little gang aren't here. I want to enjoy myself tonight.

Alexa, Olivia, and I danced around the live drum circle that was performing, but as the band heated up, so did the crowd, and I began to sweat and feel overwhelmed. I needed out.

"Alexa, I need some space. I am heading outside for a bit," I called out to her, trying to be heard over the drumming.

"Okay. Do you want us to come with you?" Alexa asked, looking concerned.

"I just need some fresh air. I'll be right back!"

"Okay, Bella!" Alexa yelled back while she continued to dance.

I immediately headed towards the side exit for some sweet, refreshing air.

I did a quick look around for my parents to let them know I was going outside but didn't see them. Maybe dressing up as Morrigan was not such a great idea considering how warm the evening was.

I finally pushed through the crowd and walked out of the side doors of the community centre.

Phew! I thought.

I reached up to blot the sweat on my forehead but remembered my face was covered in paint. *Oh well, I'll just have to let the air dry it.* I looked out at the forested ravine in front of me. It was so quiet and peaceful, even with the muffled drumming coming out of the community centre. The peace only lasted a moment, because I soon became aware that I was out there all by myself. Something about that realization made me nervous. I turned around quickly to go back into the community centre, but the doors wouldn't budge; they were locked. Panicking, I started banging on them. Nobody could hear me—the music and the roar of the crowd were too loud.

Suddenly, I felt a shiver run up my spine. Was it my imagination or was I getting cold?

It gets cold. That's normal. Totally normal, I said to myself, trying to remain calm, but I got that feeling on the back of my neck that someone was watching me.

My anxiety worsened as I began to feel prickles in my stomach. Instead of trying to convince myself that this was also a normal feeling, I decided to leave the locked entryway and creep down the stairs towards the woods where I could see if anyone else was around. As I tip-toed towards the trees, I thought I saw somebody skulking behind a cluster of bushes, so I quickly decided to turn back to the community centre and run towards the front of the building to the main entrance. As I turned the corner, a figure was standing right there! I almost ran right into it! I was initially startled by this unexpected meeting but then composed myself and went into self-defence mode.

I thought to myself, Thank goodness for all those Taekwondo lessons!

With my guard up, I called out to the figure. "Oh yeah, you don't scare me! Who are you?" I asked, trying to mask the fear in my voice.

The figure was silent, which creeped me out even more. It stood there motionless in a black and white skeleton costume.

Why wasn't anyone else around? I thought to myself.

I called out again to the skeleton, "Stop fooling around!"

I stared it up and down. Its eyes looked entirely black. Those are pretty cool special effects contact lenses. I definitely want to get a pair. It would look cool with my next Halloween costume. I shook my head. Focus on what is going on now! I reprimanded myself in my head. I got distracted so easily, even in times of danger.

My focus went back to the skeleton. The way it stood there reminded me of one of the boys in my class at school. One I did not like or trust one bit. He was friends with Rachelle, who bullied me all the time.

Forget this! I said to myself.

I straightened up out of my defensive stance and started to walk back towards the side doors I had come out of. I turned to see if he was following me, but he was gone. I whipped my head back around to continue heading towards the side of the building, and to my complete shock, he was right in front of me! I jerked backwards, feeling like I'd had a minor heart attack. *How did he move so quickly?*

"Theom, is that you? Did Rachelle put you up to this? Where is she?"

I took a quick look around, but I didn't see anyone else in the vicinity. The skeleton stood there, unflinching. He continued to stare at me with those black pits for eyes.

"Okay, your scare tactic didn't work. I am heading back in!" I said as I turned around again to go back to the front door this time.

The figure did not react at all as I walked away. Not one word was uttered. I looked down at my costume and smoothed out some of my feathers, and when I looked back up, there he was again! I jumped back in surprise.

That's it!

The pretend bravery and calmness were gone, and I made a run for it, prepared to bulldoze him if I had to. I raced by him to the doors of the centre. As I pushed past him, the strong smell of rotting eggs filled my nostrils. *Was that sulphur I was smelling?* I kept running until I made it to the doors and started banging on them as hard as I could.

"Hello! Can somebody let me in?" I called out desperately.

As I was pounding my fists against the doors, I looked over my shoulder. Skeleton boy had removed his mask. It *was* Theom! And yet, there was something odd about him. He was motionless, and his eyes were still completely black. No whites or pupils could be seen in his endless eye sockets.

I shouted at him, "Go away and leave me alone! I have my red belt in Taekwondo! I will take you down!"

Theom continued to stand there, unmoving, studying me. I noticed the air around me turn even colder.

Then, as if the cold wasn't enough to make me quake, I heard a voice say, "I finally found you, child."

I spun my head around to see who had spoken. It wasn't Theom. The voice was way too close! *Did someone just talk to me in my head?*

Before I got a chance to figure out where the voice had come from, I was distracted by the squawking of a raven. It was sitting on a tree branch above Theom.

What the frack? I said to myself. I felt cold beads of sweat on my forehead. I turned my attention back to the door, shaking it with all my might, my panic rising. It rose so high it almost reached my throat. I was ready to scream for help when, finally, I felt the door release, and I fell into the doorway and into my mom. She stood there, looking at me perplexedly. I let out a sigh of relief and quickly grabbed hold of her in a big hug.

"Oh my God, girl, I was so worried! I was looking everywhere for you!" Mom said frantically.

"I got stuck out here, and Theom was creepy over there—he was freaking me out," I babbled anxiously to my mom, pointing my finger back in the direction I had come from. I felt some relief when I noticed the air had warmed up again.

"What? I don't see anybody!" Mom glanced behind me outside of the doors.

I turned around to check for myself. Theom was gone. *Where did he go? Ugh. So creepy.* I shook my head, trying to forget the last few minutes.

"Are you okay? Why are you so cold?" Mom asked, rubbing my body with her arms to warm me up.

"Yeah, I'm okay. I guess I was scared." I did not want to tell her everything, as I did not understand it myself.

As Mom closed the front doors behind us, I turned around to take one more look back through the door window. There, staring back at me, was the raven. It was sitting on the stair railing, squawking.

I looked down at my feathers. *Had I annoyed the raven?*

The raven walked along the railing, inching closer to the front door. I stared back in astonishment out the window.

Did the raven just wink at me?

But before I could get a better look, it flew off into the darkening sky as twilight became cloaked in darkness for the night.

What a weird evening. I squeezed my mom's hand tightly as we walked through the gym doors together and back to the festival. As we walked through the crowd, I got an uneasy feeling that something was about to happen. Something was coming for me.

I

DISAPPEARING ACT—JUNE 28TH, 3:10 PM

Eager to get out of school, I shoved everything from my locker into my backpack. Scarlett and Alexa were standing next to me, texting on their phones while they waited. Olivia helped me by holding my bag open as I jammed every last remnant of the school year into my book bag. Finally, the last paintbrush was hurriedly swept inside, and I stood back to look at the empty locker. Somehow, I didn't feel as relieved as I thought I would for summer break to begin.

I knew I had to ask the others. "Did anything weird happen to you the other night at the Summer Solstice Festival?" I asked nervously.

The three girls shook their heads no.

Olivia responded, "Not really. I mean, some of the boys were trying to hit on me, but they weren't even cute! Why do you ask?"

"Hard to explain." I decided to keep my story to myself since they didn't seem to know what I was talking about. I looked around and realized this would be the last time we walked these hallways. They seemed so much smaller now.

Scarlett tugged on my backpack. "Let's get out of here."

Together, we walked down the hallway and through the front door of the school. We heard the school bell behind us; it sounded like a dying trumpet. Finally, the school year had ended!

The summer was already proving to be humid. I felt my armpits dampening from sweat. *Wow, I've got to remember to put on my deodorant. Some parts of this growing-up thing were not cool.* I held my arms down at my sides to prevent anybody from noticing. I knew I looked stiff as a soldier, but it was better than letting them see my sweat stains.

Together, we all walked home: Olivia, Alexa, Scarlett, and I. We lived only a block from the school in the neighbourhood that we had all grown up in.

Alexa, the dreamer of the group, dropped back a few steps behind us so she could whistle to herself. She was probably creating a new song, so we knew better than to bother her. Soon, Alexa's humming drifted off into the distance as I became lost in my thoughts, hoping our friendship wouldn't change when we got to high school.

I felt Olivia tap my arm. She knew I liked to daydream a lot. Olivia was the only one in our group who really got me. She understood my attention and focus problems, and she was patient when I read slowly in class because of my dyslexia, but she also knew that I could draw, paint, or doodle for hours. *She is the best . . .*

"Hey!" I said, my thoughts interrupted by a sharp jab in my shoulder.

I looked over at Olivia, who smiled apologetically. "Well, at least now you won't be bullied by Rachelle anymore," Olivia said with a soft voice, not wanting to remind me of Rachelle, but being supportive at the same time.

"I know it's just because I learn differently, and it's easy for her to pick on me because it's hard for me to stand up for myself," I responded, wanting to move past this subject.

Scarlett jumped in and said, "Well, what doesn't break you, makes you stronger or something like that."

Scarlett put her arms around Olivia's and my shoulders, and quickly, Alexa jumped in beside us. We all walked in tandem, as if we were walking down the yellow brick road, each in constant chatter over one another.

It was beautiful to have friends who appreciated me and stuck up for me when I couldn't do it myself. Rachelle always bullied me because I had to leave class for extra tutoring. I just didn't understand why she hated me so much. Even saying her name got me so flustered. Scarlett always said that I was too sensitive and that I needed to be more assertive, but I figured I wouldn't have to do that if everybody just accepted everyone else for who they were.

I felt myself getting frustrated while I fumed silently over Rachelle until Scarlett came to the rescue with one of her puns. "I'd tell you a science joke, but all of them ARGON."

"Good one, Scarlett," I laughed.

As we got closer to my house, we hugged each other goodbye and went our separate ways. I noticed the front door of my house was unlocked, which meant Mom was working from home today. I felt a knot in my stomach, knowing that things were about to change since most of my friends were going to different schools. Olivia and Alexa were moving out of the city. Georgia, Lilou, and Camille, three of my other schoolmates, were transferring to a French immersion school. Scarlett was going to an art-focused high school. For me, high school was undecided. Mom talked about homeschooling. I hated the idea, but apparently my dad was homeschooled and it was some sort of family tradition. I knew my life was changing, and I didn't like it.

Suddenly, I felt a tug on my shirt and just about fell backwards.

"Sorry, I surprised you, Ora!" Scarlett said.

"Ah, okay, what's up?" I asked.

"I'm not sensitive like you, but I am going to miss you at school."

For a moment, I didn't know what to say.

"I'm going to miss you too, Scarlett."

"Hey, if you ever want me to hunt down Theom and Rachelle, let me know. I will pun them."

"Oh no, don't ever pun them! So much verbal pun power!" I said. We both giggled, and I hugged her.

"Thanks, Scarlett," I said, feeling grateful.

We gave each other heart hands, a symbol of our adoration for each other. As Scarlett walked away, I strolled up the stairs to my house and landed on the porch that wrapped around its front. I had lived in this house my whole life, and I had always loved how old it was. Knowing that it had been here for so long made me feel safe.

"Hi, Mom, I'm home!" I shouted cheerily as I walked in the door.

"Hi, Bella. Just finishing up some work in the office. I'll be right out; we'll order pizza tonight," she called from the other room.

"Oh, yum! Can Olivia or Scarlett come over to hang out before dinner?" I asked excitedly, and then with a little more caution in my voice, "Maybe a sleepover?"

I hoped my mom would say yes, but before she could answer, Dad walked through the front door and said happily, "Looks like we finished work at the same time, Bella."

I ran to him and gave him a big hug and repeated, "Dad, can Olivia or Scarlett come over? It's the last day of school, and I thought . . ."

Mom cut me off as she came out of the office and walked over to give us both a hug.

"How was your day at the shop, Marcus?" she asked as she put her hand on my shoulder.

"It was really slow at the shop. Not enough tourists came through to buy specialty hats. How about you?"

"I think equally as frustrating. I've lost two more artists to my new competitor that just opened up on the street!" Mom replied, looking distressed.

"Well, when you have a brilliant idea like yours, you end up being copied—not everyone is as original as you," I chimed in.

"Thanks, Bella. That means a lot," Mom said with a smile.

They started talking about boring stuff, so I slowly walked upstairs with my school bag dragging behind me. I was sure they could hear me since I banged the bag against each step of the old, creaky, wooden stairs. As I got closer to the top, I saw Lolo, my best friend and super-cat, in her usual spot at the top of the stairs. I loved her shiny black and brown coat and deep blue eyes. It was almost as if she looked through me sometimes. She always made me laugh when she drooled as she greeted me.

"I'm so happy to see you, Lolo. I missed you," I said as I patted her on the head and walked past her towards my bedroom. She got up from her place at the stairs with a stretch and followed me into the room.

I threw my school bag onto the floor and heard Mom and Dad still talking about eating pizza for dinner tonight.

"Probably going to have that horrible veggie pizza that Dad always orders. The struggle is real, Lolo." I sighed as I plopped down onto the bed.

Lying there with only my thoughts to occupy me, I realized I was already feeling bored without school consuming my every waking moment.

Wow, I managed to make it through this year. Is this how adults feel when they finish college? I started worrying about the inevitability of growing up and having to make my own decisions. Thankfully my thoughts were interrupted when I heard my cell phone buzz.

I dragged myself to my backpack and noticed a message from Alexa:

Hey, do you want to go bowling tonight?

All of a sudden, I was not tired anymore, and I texted her back: Let me ask my mom and see if she can drive.

I was too lazy to walk downstairs, so I texted both Mom and Dad to see who I got a response from.

Hi, can I go bowling with Alexa tonight? Or can Scarlett or Olivia come over for a sleepover? It's the last day of school. I asked one more time, knowing they couldn't ignore a text.

I lay back down on my bed and felt Lolo jump up and snuggle on my stomach. She started to purr and drool on my shirt as I waited for a response. My cell phone buzzed. It was Mom.

Why don't we go bowling on Sunday evening with all of the girls instead? Let's just hang tonight with pizza and a movie. It's been a long week for all of us. We can sleep in and go over our summer schedule tomorrow since you're already signed up for camps.

I was disappointed because I wanted to do something tonight. It was great hanging out with the parents, but I knew the summer would fly by, and I would hardly get to see my friends. I let out a loud, defeated exhale and texted back: Okay.

I texted Olivia, Scarlett, and Alexa back that my mom would take us to the bowling alley on Sunday night.

Scarlett responded first: It's not how you bowl, it's how you roll. I'm in.

Alexa was next: For sure, I'm in.

I waited, but nothing came from Olivia.

I sent a text back to the chat room, not waiting to hear from Olivia. Awesome, bowling is on.

I put my phone down and picked up the book on my nightstand that I was reading. It was about my heroine, Amelia Earhart. I wondered what she would have done when she was my age. *Would she have wished to visit Paris and the Eiffel Tower as I did? She would have been a cool friend to have.* I heard my dad call out, breaking me out of my daydream.

"Pizza's here!"

I slowly walked downstairs and flopped onto the couch. As usual, it was tough for us to choose a movie we wanted to watch. I wanted a horror movie, Dad wanted a classic film, and Mom wanted a romantic comedy. Since we could not decide, we ended up playing "Shoe-opoly," a board game that my dad made for me on my tenth birthday because my mom and I both love shoes.

I always chose Dorothy's red slippers as my board piece, Mom always wanted Cinderella's slipper, and poor Dad was left with the ballet shoe. Dad always said he would make more shoe pieces for us, but he was so busy at the store that it had yet to happen. That was the life of entrepreneurial parents, but from the sound of it, it was tough work owning your own business. This sort of made me sad, because at times it felt like I was competing with their work for their attention.

The main goal of the game was to build an empire of shoe stores. My mom and I were the competitive ones of the family, but between turns, I doodled in my comic strip book, coming up with new characters for my superhero comic.

We inhaled the pepperoni pizza—my fave—and before we knew it, it was 11:00 PM. I got ready for bed while Mom and Dad cleaned up, but as I was brushing my teeth, I heard the cawing of a raven outside the bathroom window. Shivers went through my body, thinking back to what happened at the community centre the other night. I spat out my toothpaste and ignored it, trying to continue my bedtime routine: pyjamas on and a hug from Mom.

"Good night, Bella," Mom said, appearing at the open bathroom door. "Have you thought any further about being homeschooled in the fall?"

"Mom, it's so late. I'm tired," I replied, trying to avoid this conversation.

"Well, we need to talk about it soon. We don't want to miss out on signing you up for a high school if you decide you don't want to do it."

Dad walked in, and I thought to myself, *Wow, are we having a bathroom party?*

"As much as I hate the idea myself, we don't want to break from tradition. Your mom is right about homeschooling. We could plan trips for learning purposes," Dad offered hopefully.

Mom looked at Dad with a strange grin.

I had no idea what that look meant, but I was not going to make a decision tonight.

"But when are you guys going to have time to do that when you're so busy already?"

"We'll make time." Mom and Dad jinxed each other.

Mom smiled at me one more time before she exited the bathroom, and Dad took the extra space to lean forward to give me a hug goodnight. I held him tightly in the embrace, feeling loved and warm and understood.

But as I stood there, knowing the true meaning of comfort, I froze as the warmth drained right out of me. I could feel my dad's arms still around me, but it was like cold steel, and I was trapped within it. It was a flash, like a memory. I was a ghost that nobody could see.

I stood there, paralyzed. I felt so cold and alone, yet I could sense a shadow in the background. It was calling out to me, but I couldn't make out what the voice was saying. I trembled as I stood there, awash in the cold and the fear, but the feeling faded as quickly as it came, and I was safely in my father's arms once again. All that remained was the awful feeling that something was going to happen. I held onto my dad even tighter.

"Whoa, that's quite the bear hug," Dad said.

Dad let go of me and winked as he left the bathroom and headed off to his and Mom's bedroom.

I finished up in the bathroom and walked to my room, ignoring the terrifying experience I had just imagined. Lolo was already on top of my bedsheets, looking at me. I hesitated for a moment, not sure if I should close my bedroom door or not, but I decided to anyway. Then, I went over to my bedroom curtains to close them. It was way too hot to close the window, but I didn't want any more scary run-ins with ravens.

I was tired, so I lay down next to Lolo on the bed, but before I could allow myself to doze off, I called out to my mom and dad one more time to put my mind at ease. They responded with a final, "Good night!" and I could finally slip into sleep.

I couldn't have been asleep for very long, but I already felt myself dreaming a dream I had experienced a thousand times before: I dreamt of a falcon and a tree.

I thought it was normal to have the same dream over and over, but when I told Scarlett, Olivia, and Alexa about

Nothing but silence. The bedroom lamp lights stopped flickering and returned to their normal steady glow. The smell of sulphur was gone. Their bed was empty.

I ran back to my room, grabbed my cell phone, and began to look for Opa's phone number. My hands were shaking as I scrolled through the contact list. I got frustrated when I could not find it right away, but Lolo had calmed down and was purring at my feet, which helped me to steady my racing thoughts. Finally, I found it and dialed the number. The phone kept ringing and ringing.

"Please, answer the phone!" I yelled out of fear and frustration.

A voice finally picked up. "Hello, who is this?"

"Opa, this is Orabella! I need your help! Dad and Mom disappeared into thin air!"

There was silence on the other end. "Bella, are you okay?"

"No, Opa, I'm freaking out! What's going on? Where did they go?"

"Orabella, I'm going to call your Auntie Adri. She's going to pick you up and bring you here."

"What do you mean? Why can't I stay with Auntie? She lives so close, and you live so far away!" I was holding back from full-on screaming into the phone.

"Orabella, you need to come here. I can explain what is going on."

"How did Mom and Dad just disappear into thin air like that? It was like a crazy sci-fi movie! Were they kidnapped by aliens?" I frantically asked, my imagination going wild.

"Orabella, I'm calling your aunt now. She'll be there in a few minutes."

I started to cry as I hung up.

So weird. Opa seemed so calm.

I was still in shock. I was about to text my friends but remembered I still had to go to the bathroom. I really needed to pee now. As I washed my hands, I heard my cell phone ring. I quickly picked up the phone.

"Hi, Bella, it's Auntie Adri. I'm on my way! Are you okay?"

"Please hurry. I'm scared," I whispered as I felt a shiver run through my body. I began to cry again.

"Okay, I'll be there as soon as I can," Auntie said in a calm voice.

I could hear her car door close while she was talking to me.

"Bella, please don't tell anybody about this."

"Okay, Auntie, but I'm terrified and confused. My mom and dad just vanished!"

"Orabella, I'm in the car and on the way. Head downstairs."

I lost her connection and tried calling her back, but there was no answer.

I grabbed Lolo and ran downstairs, waiting for my aunt at the front door, scared and alone. I looked out the window. All of the neighbours' windows were dark, including the bedrooms of Olivia and Scarlett, who lived just across the street. I guess that was a good thing; I wouldn't have to explain why I was up.

2

ANCIENT FOREST—JUNE 29TH, 3:15 AM

It felt like I waited by the door for hours. Every groan the old house made seemed louder than usual, as if it were talking to me. I saw the headlights of a car pull into the driveway, and I immediately knew it was Auntie. I ran to the car to meet her. I had not seen Auntie in a while, but, being my mom's twin, there was immediately a feeling of recognition and safety. They both had the same brown hair that I did, but my mom kept hers long, and Auntie always cut hers short in a bob. I gave her the biggest hug and did not want to let go of that feeling of comfort. I was glad to have her there with me.

I finally pulled away from her. "Auntie, where did they go? They just disappeared into thin air!"

"Orabella, I spoke with Oma and Opa, and they think it best if you stay with them."

"Why can't I stay with you?" I pled with her through chattering teeth as an uncontrollable panic ran through me.

"Orabella, you're on summer break, and I need to work during the day. Opa and Oma will look after you for now."

"You don't understand! They just disappeared before my eyes! How can you be so calm? I don't understand what's happening! Shouldn't we call the police?"

Auntie responded dismissively, "Opa will explain everything when you get there."

I was so frustrated by the lack of answers I was being given. "Auntie, why aren't you telling me what's going on?"

"You need to trust us and know everything will be okay. Opa will explain why they disappeared. Come on, let's go." Auntie walked towards the house and I followed. "Your grandparents don't live that far away. I can come and get you if you decide you hate it there. Besides, your mom and I grew up there with your dad. It's not that bad!"

"Oh yeah I forgot about that. Mom hardly mentions it."

"Come on, let's go pack your suitcase."

As we climbed the stairs to my bedroom, I felt a dread that my life would never be the same again. I remained quiet as Auntie helped me pack a couple of suitcases. It appeared that I would be staying for a while. I put Lolo into the cat carrier. She was unusually eager to leave the house. *What is she so anxious about?* As we walked out of my bedroom, I took one last glance back at my parents' room. It was empty and dark.

Auntie tried to keep her tone light as we locked up the house. "It's only a short ride from here to the ferry terminal. We'll catch the first ferry over, and then it's a short drive to their place."

I remained quiet as we drove away from the house. I took one last look back, fearing I wouldn't see it again for a long while. *Is that? It couldn't be.* It almost looked as if there was a dark figure standing in my parents' bedroom, outlined by the flickering of lamp lights. My panic began to rise again. I blinked. The room was as empty and dark as I had left it.

I turned back around and knew I needed to be distracted. "So, what was it like living with Dad?" I asked.

"Well, we were fifteen when our parents died. Oma and Opa were our godparents, so your mom and I moved in with them."

I knew it was still hard for them to talk about losing their parents, even after all this time, but I was so shaken by the evening's events that I needed Auntie to keep talking.

"Did you guys get along?"

"When we first moved in, we hardly saw your dad, as he was mostly off doing his own stuff, but then around his 19th birthday, he began to grow fond of your mom. That's when they started dating and kept it a secret from Oma and Opa."

"Really? How long did they keep it a secret?"

"Oh, for almost a year. Then your dad went off to college in the city, and your mom soon followed him after she graduated."

"Were you guys all friends?"

"Well, for whatever reason, your dad and I did not get along. Maybe it was because your mom ended up spending more time with your dad than with me, but we had a lot of different opinions about things. Your dad can be stubborn at times."

"Yeah, I think I got that trait from him." I laughed.

"Well, that is not the only thing you got from him. I can't believe how tall you've gotten!" My aunt exclaimed, looking at me in the passenger seat. I had outgrown my aunt and my mom just this year.

"Yeah, I am one of the tallest in my class, but I'm so clumsy too," I said, a little bit embarrassed.

"Yes, one of the traits on your dad's side for sure, but you'll grow out of it," my aunt said with a smile.

We both became quiet. I watched the street lamps pass by on the highway, and it felt like we were the only ones on the road as we headed towards the ferry terminal. I was hypnotized by the passing lights as I stared out the window. Suddenly my trance was cut by a vision, almost as if it were a memory. It was my grandfather, rolling down a hill, screaming. *Help me.*

My stomach knotted up. I sometimes got flashes foretelling a gruesome future, like when Scarlett fell off her skateboard and broke her ankle. I warned her of what I had seen, but she ignored me, and the next day she was getting a cast put on her ankle. After that incident, Scarlett never looked at me the same way again. I decided I would never mention these visions in the future. I hoped that this flash of Opa was nothing more than my nerves getting the best of me. I didn't want to think about it any longer, so I returned my focus to the passing lights.

We finally arrived at the ferry terminal and were the first in line. Auntie and I stayed in the car with the windows halfway down. My eyes were burning from crying earlier, and I could taste the dried salt on my cheeks. I kept looking down at my cell phone. It was 4:55 in the morning. *Should I text Olivia or Scarlett? What do I say to them? How do I explain to them what happened when I don't even know?*

The air was crisp as the sun rose over the mountains, but I could feel the warmth of the sun heating the air. I felt confused, frustrated, and angry, yet calm knowing I would soon see my grandparents. Opa was my father's dad. Both of my grandparents were born in Zundert, Holland where they met and married. My great-grandfather was a shoemaker there, like many of his ancestors before him.

I had never visited my grandparents' home. The last time I saw them was when they came to visit us in Vancouver for my 8th birthday. My dad and Opa had not spoken much since then. I think they got into a fight, but I never knew what it was about. When they would come to visit us, they would tell us stories of their childhood. Holland seemed like a faraway, magical place with bright, colourful fields of tulips and big windmills.

I felt a knot in my stomach again, and I started to shiver. I asked Auntie a question to continue the distractions. "Auntie, have you been to Holland?"

She looked at me. "Yes, when your mom and dad got married. Holland is stunning."

"What is Oma and Opa's place like? I've never been," I asked nervously.

"You may find it a little boring, but it's a beautiful place, and it'll be nice to get out of Vancouver for a while and spend time with your grandparents."

"Well, I hope it's not for too long. I'm supposed to go fishing with my dad next week." I tried to stay hopeful that life would return to normal again, and soon.

Auntie didn't answer, which only made me more nervous as the car boarded the ferry. We got out of the car to stretch our legs and headed to the upper deck. There were only a few people on board. We found a seat, and I decided to ask again, "What do you think happened to Mom and Dad?"

"Bella, it's complicated. I know you're scared and worried, but your answers will have to come from Opa."

"But why can't you tell me? Why is it so hard? I just don't understand how they could disappear like that, and that weird smell . . ."

"What weird smell?"

"The smell of rotten eggs, and the lights were blinking too!"

"All good questions to ask Opa. Okay, let's get back to the car. We're nearing the terminal."

"Wow, that was quick."

"Yes, it's not too far, only about twenty minutes by ferry."

We got back in the car and buckled in. I looked over at Auntie and almost begged her to tell me what was going on, so I wouldn't freak out. Even though she looked just like my mom, she just didn't have the same warmth and sympathy that my mom always provided. Auntie looked over at me and saw the tears running down my face that I had tried to hold back since leaving the house.

"Oh, Bella." She unbuckled her seatbelt and leaned over to hug me. "Trust me; everything will be okay."

"But all I want is my mom and dad to be back. I just want to wake up from this bad dream."

She continued to hug me, and I cried until the ferry docked, and even after Auntie started the car and drove off the ferry onto the road, she held my hand tightly.

The roads were winding, and as we headed further up the coast, there was less traffic and fewer houses. Then we finally arrived at their home, which was settled in a valley between two mountains. There were two houses and a shed on their property. The big house was white with blue trim, and it had a wraparound porch, just like our house in Vancouver. I loved the smaller blue house in the back that looked like a mini barn. It looked older than the main house, and it was very quaint. Between the two houses grew an unusual tree that I had never seen before. Its trunk was massive, and its branches grew only at the top, reaching towards the sky. Behind the houses, I could see a small river that twisted around the back of the property.

"What you may find boring here is that Oma and Opa live off the grid," Auntie said.

I was not quite sure what that meant, but I didn't care at that point. I wanted to know what happened to my parents.

My grandparents were both out on the porch when we arrived. It had been a while since I had seen them last. I had forgotten how tall Oma and Opa were, and they both had gotten more grey hair. I barely got myself out of the car when Oma ran up to me and caught me in a big hug.

"Oh, my! Orabella, you have grown so much! You're not a little girl anymore! Right, Opa?" Oma asked him.

"Yes indeed, Audrey, she has grown so much," Opa said and came over to hug me.

Oma and Opa bent down to say hello to Lolo in her carrier, and I could hear her purring excitedly.

Opa walked over to Auntie to greet her, but she turned to avoid his embrace.

"Jasper, you need to tell Orabella everything. Now is the time," Auntie told him sternly.

"Yes, Adri, I know, but it's a lot to tell a girl her age."

"Hey, I'm right in front of you!" I demanded as I pulled away from Oma, who was holding me by my shoulders. "I need to know what happened to my mom and dad! How could they have disappeared like that?"

The tension between Auntie and Opa was noticeable, but I didn't care. I needed to know.

"Why haven't we called the police to help? This is crazy!" I yelled.

Oma and Opa looked at me in disbelief but still said nothing.

Then, my cell phone buzzed in my hand, and I looked down to see that Olivia was texting me:

I came by to say hi, but you were gone. Is anybody home?

I quickly texted back, I'm visiting my grandparents.

My phone buzzed again.

When will you be back? My parents surprised me with a European vacation. The first stop is Holland. So excited, leaving tomorrow! Olivia texted.

Seriously, why is everybody going to Holland while I'm stuck in this uneventful place? I shouted in my head.

I overheard Auntie say to Opa and Oma, "This girl deserves to know the truth about who she is. No more secrets."

Oma then spoke to me, and I heard her slight Dutch accent, "Let's get your luggage into the house. We'll sit down at the kitchen table and talk about it."

What secrets? I was angry that nobody was saying anything, but I felt sick from worrying about my mom and dad. We sat at the kitchen table while Opa made tea. Auntie and Oma sat across from me in a way that told me a lecture was about to happen. Suddenly, all I wanted to do was go to my room and hide. I needed to find comfort somewhere. I needed to feel safe.

I heard the kettle whistle behind me, and Opa brought over four cups of tea and set them down at the end of the table.

A draft came through the open window, a clean smell that we didn't get back in Vancouver. I was starving, but I just wanted to go to bed. I began to yawn.

"Orabella, you look tired. A lot has happened. Maybe you should go have a nap. When you're ready, Opa and I will tell you everything," Oma said.

I was eager to know what happened to my mom and dad, but fatigue fought against me.

"Okay, Oma, but no more secrets when I wake up," I said as I looked at Opa who was nodding his head in agreement.

I grabbed Lolo's carrier as I followed Oma on our way to the spare bedroom. When we got there, the room was nice and cozy with big, fluffy pillows on the bed. Oma put my luggage down, and I released Lolo, who immediately leapt up on the bed and made herself comfortable. I scratched behind her ears for a moment, and then my attention was brought to the large tree outside the window. It was the tree that I saw when I arrived. It stood right outside of my bedroom window, looming over the house with an air of protection, as if its branches were huddling over it to keep us safe. As I looked out at the tree, a sense of calm washed over me. I couldn't help but think that this tree looked almost exactly like the tree in my dreams.

3
MONKEY TREE

"Oma, what kind of tree is that?" I asked.

"That is an African Baobab," Oma answered, walking up to gaze out the window. "Your great-grandfather planted the seed when he first arrived back in 1925. These types of trees can live for up to five thousand years."

"I've never seen a tree with such a huge trunk," I said in amazement.

"In Africa, each tree can grow as high as thirty meters, and its trunk can grow to fifty meters in diameter. Baobab trees can provide shelter, food, and water for animals and humans, which is why many savannah communities have made their homes near them."

"That's cool," I said with a tired voice.

"The coolest part is that many cultures around the world consider it to be the Tree of Life."

"What's the Tree of Life?" I asked despite my exhaustion.

"The Tree of Life is a common myth. In most cultures, they believe that it connects heaven and earth and everything in between. It's also called the World Tree or Cosmic Tree, and all living things are connected to it."

"How do you know so much about the tree, Oma?" I asked, eager to learn more.

"Well, you remember I used to be a history teacher. I can't help but love studying old myths and cultures."

I suddenly started to feel dizzy and allowed myself to fall back into the bed.

Oma kissed me on the forehead and said, "Get some rest. Your mom and dad are okay. There is a lot for you to learn while you're here, so when you're ready, come downstairs." She turned and walked out the door, closing it shut behind her.

While I lay there, Lolo jumped up to settle herself in her usual sleeping spot on my stomach. She started purring immediately. I could hear my aunt and grandparents talking downstairs in the kitchen through the heating vent.

"Jasper, you and Audrey have been like family to me," Auntie said. "You helped raise Mary and me. You shared your secret as to who you and Marcus were. But when Bella was born, we all knew from the beginning that this was different than anything else you'd ever experienced. You need to tell her everything—now."

"Adri, I agree with you," Opa said, "but it's Marcus who fights me over it. That was one of the reasons we stopped talking. Five years ago, he got mad at me after I suggested that Orabella come to stay with us."

"I don't care what happened then. Orabella needs to know what has happened to her parents," Adri said sternly.

"Adri, I hear you, but I think we should get her settled in before we reveal things to her. Otherwise, she might reject it all," Oma said with frustration.

"Well, I need to get back to Vancouver. I've got work tomorrow," Auntie huffed.

I could hear the chairs squeak against the floor as they stood up from the table.

"I need to put things into action at Marcus's hat shop and Mary's gift store. There's a lot to do. I don't want anybody to get suspicious, especially the police. How would you explain all of this to anybody outside of this family?" Auntie scoffed.

"Adri, I know you've never been happy about knowing our family secret, but it's your family too. Especially after Mary and Marcus fell in love, we had no choice but to tell you. We're happy you brought Bella; it's been a while since you visited," Oma replied calmly.

"It's so hard to know the truth and live in a world that I know isn't real. It messes me up, and the only person I can talk to about it is Mary, but she barely talks to me these days! But no matter what, I want my sister back, and I blame you for taking her away from me, Jasper!" Adri yelled. "You're both in your seventies now. It's time for that girl upstairs to know the truth before something happens to you!"

I was shocked at what I heard. *What was this great secret?* I listened to my aunt close the front door, and I jumped up and ran to the window to wave goodbye. She looked up at me and returned the wave, and I felt sad as I watched her car disappear down the road. Well, this was the start of an eventful summer break. I lay back down on the bed, thinking about what had happened, but I soon dozed off into a deep sleep.

Oma came up to wake me from my nap. "Orabella, lunch is ready. You should eat something to keep your strength up," she said softly.

I looked at my phone. I had napped for two hours. I looked at Oma standing in the doorway. She was wearing a brightly coloured shirt and the same jeans she always wore. Her face was kind and beautiful, barely lined despite so many years of tending to her garden in the sunlight.

I responded groggily, "Oma, I'm not hungry, and I'm still so tired. Can I nap a little longer?"

"Okay, let me at least bring up a sandwich for you. I made BLTs."

"I love BLTs," I said, perking up a little bit.

Oma returned a few minutes later with a glass of water and the bacon, lettuce, and tomato sandwich. She left them on the desk by the window.

"Eat what you can. When you're ready, just come downstairs."

"Will do, Oma. Thank you," I replied.

After Oma left, Opa appeared in the doorway with a book in his hands.

"Bella, I know this is difficult, but I need you to look through these books of old photos and tell me if you recognize any of these people. It will help me understand more about what happened to your parents," Opa said.

"How is this going to help my parents? Opa, they DISAPPEARED INTO THIN AIR! That is not normal!" My anger grew at the lack of direct answers from my grandfather.

"Please, Bella, this will help me out a lot, and you're right—disappearing is not normal, which is why this is so important."

Opa seemed worried and sincere, so I took a deep breath and calmly took the photo album from his hands. I flipped through it. There were mostly old pictures of different people, places, and what appeared to be different times. There was one with a woman wearing a 50's dress pushing a baby carriage. I looked up, but Opa was gone. I felt so confused, but I continued to look through the book.

I sat down on the floor next to my bed and slowly examined each picture while I inhaled my sandwich. As I flipped photo after photo, one stood out to me: a black and white picture of an old car and what looked like my dad standing next to it, but that wasn't possible. It wasn't like my dad was wearing regular clothes and standing next to someone else's old car. It looked like he fit the time period entirely. I also noticed him holding a book or a journal in one hand, but it looked modern. It did not fit into the time period. *Weird.* I made a mental note of the photo to tell Opa about it and then moved on to the next picture.

As I searched through the book, Lolo was curled up next to me, purring. In between petting Lolo and looking over the photos, I checked my phone, hoping for messages from my friends. I wanted some semblance of normalcy in my life to continue to exist, but no messages ever came.

I wasn't sure how much time had passed, but when I finally finished the book, the sun was starting to set, and I realized I seriously needed to take a bath. I got up to look around for Oma and Opa, but they were nowhere to be found. I headed into the bathroom, figuring I would see them when I got out.

I loved the old-fashioned clawed bathtub that Oma and Opa had in their bathroom. Everything in their house was either antique or vintage. It was busy but homey and thoughtfully decorated. After my bath, I dried myself off, wrapped the towel around me, and went back to my bedroom. I noticed that Oma and Opa's bedroom door was closed. When I got back to my room, I saw a pair of old pyjamas on my bed and a note that said:

Hi Bella, I hope you're feeling better. This is a pair of pyjamas your mom used to wear, and I thought you might like to wear them tonight. Opa and I have gone to bed, as we are normally up early to get started on chores. Sleep well, and see you for breakfast.

Love, Oma.

How odd that they didn't wait for me to get out of the bath to say goodnight. Mom and Dad would never have done that. I put on Mom's pyjamas. They were soft and comforting—like she was there with me. I opened my luggage to pull out my favourite stuffed animal when a picture of my mom and dad fell out. I stared at them and tasted the salt of my tears. I was already feeling so homesick. I thought about my friends back home and wondered when I would see them again. How long would I be here? When would Mom and Dad come to pick me up?

Oh no, I forgot to text the girls back to tell them that we wouldn't be going bowling. It seemed so trivial now, but I didn't want to make anyone suspicious by leaving them hanging without any notice.

I texted but received no immediate reply, which made me even sadder. I felt so alone. I jumped under the covers and cried as I held my stuffed raccoon close, wishing I was back in my own bed at home.

Where are you, Mom and Dad? I miss you.

Lolo jumped up and cuddled next to me as I fell asleep with tears running down my cheeks.

That night, for the first time in a long time, I had a different kind of dream. I dreamt about my parents being taken away. I ran after them, but something held me back. There were shoes everywhere, and my parents were getting further and further away from me. No matter how fast I ran, I couldn't get to them. I woke with a start from Oma, who was gently shaking me to wake up.

Immediately I felt confused. *Where am I?*

When Oma noticed I was awake, she stopped shaking me and said, "Orabella, you can't sleep all day. Breakfast is ready. We have lots of chores to do."

Finally, my eyes focused on her, and I remembered where I was.

She smiled at me and coaxed me with some food. "Come on, we'll eat before we get started for the day." She gave me one last pat on my shoulder to make sure I stayed awake then walked out of the room.

What kind of chores am I supposed to do? Uggggghhhh.

I rolled out of bed begrudgingly and took some clothes out of my suitcase, slowly mulling over what to wear. But, when the smell of breakfast wafted past my nose, my attitude quickly changed. I put on whatever was nearest and ran out of the bedroom, grabbing my phone on my way out. I needed a charger. Hopefully, Oma and Opa would have one. As I got closer to the bottom of the stairs, my hunger only intensified at the smell of homemade pancakes, warm syrup, and bacon. I started drooling in anticipation.

I rushed through the house to the kitchen and saw Oma flipping some pancakes over the stove, but it didn't distract me from my question. I quickly went to Oma.

"Oma, do you have a cell phone charger I could use? My phone is about to die."

She turned her head away from the stove to answer me. "Of course, dear, but I don't know that we have the same kind of phone that you do." I double-checked. They didn't.

"Okay, then do you have a computer I could use? Or could I turn on the television while I wait for breakfast?"

"I'm so sorry, Bella, but we don't have that sort of thing. If we need to use a computer, we go to the library. And if we want to watch something, we go to the local movie theatre. We normally don't use our cell phones at home because the signal is so bad."

I froze. What was I going to do? I would be so bored here! I wouldn't be able to watch my shows, play my games, or text my friends. My social life was over!

Oma was talking to me as she cooked, but I stopped listening, getting lost in my thoughts of despair. It was then that Opa came up behind me and asked, "Orabella, how did you sleep? You must be hungry. Can you set the table for breakfast?"

I nodded and looked around the kitchen for where to start. *This is not my home.* I started opening and slamming shut cupboard doors trying to look for plates and silverware. I burst out crying, feeling like I barely knew my grandparents and they barely knew me. *How could I be stuck here with them?* Oma came over to hug me, but I shrugged her away.

"Why did I have to look at all those pictures yesterday?" I exploded at Opa. Oma looked at me worriedly then went back to the stove. "Why did my mom and dad just disappear like that? Why did you not say good night to me?" I yelled at Opa in frustration.

Opa quietly responded, "Outstanding questions. You will get your answers, but there are family secrets that I need to be sure that you are ready to hear, and I need a little more time to collect all the information that needs to be told. In the meantime, we need your help around the house."

I huffed audibly. "Why can't you just tell me now?"

Opa did not respond. Instead, as if he didn't know I was furious with him, he walked over to one of the cabinets and pulled out three plates and set them down on the table. Then he looked up at me calmly and asked, "Did you recognize anybody from the photo album I gave you yesterday?"

I fumed for a moment before I responded, "No. I looked through it several times, but I only recognized Dad standing by an old car, like he had travelled back in time." For some reason, I did not mention the book in his hand.

"Orabella, your parents are safe, there's no need to be angry."

I couldn't stop myself. "I don't understand what you're not telling me!" I yelled. "It's hard for me to trust you when I feel like you're hiding things from me!"

I looked down at my cell phone. It had died. "I need a charger!"

With my last lifeline to home gone, I began to cry into my hands. Opa came over and hugged me. I pushed away from his embrace at first, but then gave in and hugged him back. I was tired of crying, and I was hungry. I guess I would have to wait a little longer to find out where my parents had gone.

Oma set breakfast down on the table, and we all quietly sat in our chairs to eat. I felt terrible about the way I acted, but Oma and Opa were good at letting it go and quickly changed the conversation to the different chores that needed to be done: feeding the chickens, doing laundry, and painting the fence. They were happy I was here to help them out. I quickly tuned them out and started daydreaming about the trips and camps that my mom and dad had planned for the summer. I hoped my parents would come home soon. I didn't want to have to work the whole summer break.

My attention was brought back to the table as I watched—incredulously—as Opa poured ketchup on just about everything on his plate. I had forgotten how much he loved ketchup. Opa made his own from the tomatoes in their garden. It was so flavourful. The store-bought kind could never compare.

After breakfast, we washed the dishes, which was new for me because we would usually just put them in the dishwasher at home (but of course, they didn't have one of those either). As I washed the dishes and Opa dried them, he flicked soap in my face, and it soon turned into a kitchen soap fight. With my clothes soaked, I went upstairs to change into a different outfit for the day. I chose some jean shorts and a t-shirt with a cute kitten on it.

On my way back down, I stopped every few steps to look at the old pictures along the wall. There was one of Opa and Oma in Holland, standing by some windmills, and a picture of my aunt and my mom when they were teenagers. There were pictures of my dad and my mom together. I looked closer at a photo of Opa and Oma on vacation in London and noticed there was an odd shadow behind them that didn't seem to have any reason to be there. I then looked back at the other pictures and saw the same shadow behind Opa in all of them. I got goosebumps up my arms. There was something familiar about the shape of the shadow, but I couldn't put my finger on it.

I was interrupted by Oma's voice outside calling for me. "Orabella, can you come outside please? I want to show you around."

I walked down the rest of the stairs and out the front door to find Oma. A rush of fresh air hit me. I took a deep breath. For a second time, I noticed how much cleaner the air was here than in Vancouver.

I looked around for Oma and saw her over by the chicken coop. She waved to me to come over and help her feed the chickens. There were twelve of them. I tried to name them all, but they moved around so quickly. Eventually, I ended up picking my favourite, whom I called Betty since she was a blonde like my favourite comic book character. A stab of pain hit me as I thought of how my mom and I used to read those comics together, but I drove the sadness away quickly by staying distracted with the chickens. Betty was the only one who wouldn't run away from me when I tried to feed her.

Oma showed me where the eggs were. We were to collect them to take to the farmers market.

Oma then showed me the garden, which had squash, carrots, cucumbers, and beets. She taught me how to take care of them: plant them, turn the soil, and nurture them. It would be cool to see them grow from my efforts. I picked some carrots, beets, and lettuce to put in a salad for dinner.

The day passed by quickly since there was so much to do outside. I appreciated the distraction, but as we finished up for the day and made our way back to the house, my mind filled with the anxiety of not knowing where my parents were. When were they going to tell me what was going on? I was anxious to know what this big secret was that Auntie and Opa kept mentioning. If they were not going to tell me, then I would need to get answers for myself.

Oma interrupted my thoughts. "Tomorrow is Sunday. We need to get ready for the farmers market."

"Why do we need to go?" I asked.

"We sell eggs, jams, and veggies at the market. We need to be up early, so we'll have an early dinner and go to bed right after."

"Okay, Oma. While we're in town, I need to buy a cell phone charger, so I can check my messages. There might be some from Mom and Dad."

"Okay, Bella. Just remind me in the morning."

4

FARMERS MARKET—JULY 1ST, 6:05 AM

The rooster woke me up. At home, I would usually sleep in on Sunday. But this morning, I was up before the sunrise. We had to prepare for the farmers market, and there was a lot to do. I helped make breakfast with Oma, then collected the eggs and loaded the truck with Opa. I was excited to go to the farmer's market, which made me feel guilty because I felt like my thoughts should be solely focused on my parents' disappearance, but I couldn't help but feel a little bit of anticipation for the day.

Oma said that the market was often busy with tourists and locals looking to buy local products—very much like the stores of my mom and dad. It would be extra busy today with the Canada Day celebrations.

"Orabella, if you sell more eggs today than we did last year, I'll give you 50% of the profits," Opa said.

"Wow, thank you, Opa," I said as I thought, *Cool, I get to make some money while I'm here. So, I've officially become Orabella the Egg Seller.*

We were all set up in our booth, sandwiched between someone selling cheese and someone else who sold homemade soaps. I had been busy selling eggs all morning when there was finally a lull in the pace of customers. I was grateful to have a moment to relax, but, before I could even set my basket down, a family of three appeared at our booth. It was hard to make out who they were with the sun shining in my eyes. I opened my mouth to ask if they were interested in buying some of our eggs, but before I could even get a word out, an all too familiar voice greeted me smugly.

"Oh, it's you," one of the figures said to me with her arms folded across her chest.

I finally moved to a position where the sun wasn't glaring in my eyes, and my stomach dropped at the recognition of the one and only Rachelle. Her devilish grin was in its usual place; her long black hair shone in the sunlight and her crystal blue eyes stared at me with mockery and contention.

I couldn't believe what I was seeing. My heart pounded in my ears, and I began to sweat. It was the bully from my school who had made it a point to make my life miserable for years.

At that moment, all the feelings that had disappeared since school had ended rushed back to form a large knot in my stomach. A sense of helplessness overcame me. I didn't have any friends nearby to protect me, and I just wanted to cry. Despite the dread I felt, I stared at Rachelle with a wide grin, determined not to show her how I felt.

"What are you doing here in the market?" Rachelle asked.

I felt like I wanted to vomit, but I continued to smile instead. "Hi, I'm just helping out my grandparents."

Rachelle glanced over at her parents, who were talking to Oma and Opa, and then she looked back at me disgustedly. "I can't even. It's so basic here. I hope we're only here for the day." She looked at the basket of eggs in my hands and then took a look around the rest of the booth with disdain very apparent upon her face. I felt my cheeks go red instantly, feeling like everything I ever did was inferior to her. She continued talking, ignoring my humiliation.

"By the way, I spoke with Alexa. She's wondering why you haven't called her."

As if this moment couldn't get any worse, now Rachelle was talking badly about me to Alexa. I had been so preoccupied with finding out the family secret for the last two days that I hadn't thought about anything else. Now I was being reminded of all the bad parts about school, and I would have to worry about what rumours Rachelle was spreading to my friends back in Vancouver while I was gone.

Oma put her hand on my back as she completed the sale with Rachelle's parents. When the three of them walked away, Rachelle looked back at me with a snide glance. Then, she whipped her head back around, her long black hair swishing behind her as she and her parents walked on to another booth.

"Are you okay?" Oma asked.

"No, Oma. I want to go home."

Oma hugged me in response.

"Oma, Rachelle always makes me look bad in front of my friends. She tells lies about me. She disses me and tries to convince my friends not to spend time with me anymore. I heard there was an online chat with a group in my class that made fun of me because I learn differently. I feel all alone in the class, like I can't trust anybody, even my closest friends." I looked away and tried to rein in my emotions before I continued.

"She even told me once that I shouldn't be in the same class as her because of my dyslexia. That I should be in a special class with the rest of the special students. She always makes me feel inadequate." I started to cry.

"Orabella, do you know of the white wolf, black wolf story?"

"I think I do." I tried to hold back the tears, but there was already a steady flow rolling down my cheeks.

"It's an old Native American folk story that a friend told me many years ago. A grandfather is educating his grandson about life. He tells him that the struggle that goes on inside of each person is a black wolf and a white wolf. The white wolf represents what is right. The black wolf is what is wrong about us. The white wolf thrives on justice and peace, and the black wolf thrives on anger, fear, and hatred. The black wolf is your thoughts or a person in your life that feeds off of your negative feelings.

"And as long as she upsets you, it's a lot easier for her to feed your black wolf than your white wolf when you are affected by her opinion. If you are fearful of her, she has power over you."

Hearing this story allowed me to breathe normally again, and I caught myself thinking, *What's wrong with me?* I realized my self-doubt was feeding my black wolf and hers. Instead, my voice could be my friend. I was thankful that Oma reminded me of this tale.

"Also, remember that experiences with bullies will help you learn how to deal with those sorts of people when you're older. Bullies exist everywhere—even when you're an adult. That is why when you graduate from high school, it's important to travel. Travelling the world is an important tool for finding yourself within, for experiencing different cultures, meeting new people, and seeing the wonders of the world. This keeps the magic of life and inspires the child within you to stay wondrous."

"Thanks, Oma. You're the best," I said with a grateful smile.

The rest of the day went by without any incident, and thankfully I didn't see Rachelle again in the market. Happy with what we sold, we packed up our booth and put our remaining things in the pickup truck to head home.

"Oma, can we make French toast with whipped cream for dinner tonight?" I asked as my stomach began to growl just thinking about it. "Maybe it can be opposite day, and we can have breakfast for dinner!"

Oma replied, "That would be fun, let's make it together."

Opa shut the door of the truck and came over to where Oma and I were standing.

"Good work today, Orabella! Do you want to stay in town for the Canada Day festivals?" he asked cheerily.

"Sure, that would be cool!"

Opa locked the truck and grabbed Oma by the hand, which I thought was sweet. I walked slightly ahead since it was busy in town with all the tourists. I didn't want to stray too far in case I had another run-in with Rachelle.

We came upon a giant-sized Jenga game in the street. Opa and I started pulling blocks out and putting one on top of the other to form a precarious tower. Oma watched and called out to us, telling us which ones to pull and where to place them. We all laughed heartily as, brick after brick, our tower was still successfully upright. I squealed as I pulled out one block that I was sure was going to take the whole thing down, but I slid it out ever so gently and couldn't believe the structure didn't tip over.

But as I reached up on my tiptoes to place it atop the others, I saw through a hole in the tower a familiar face glaring at me. Our eyes met, and I dropped my block heavily in its place, causing the whole tower to come crumbling down. I backed away as it came crashing to the pavement, and I looked over at Opa in embarrassment. My eyes then darted back to the crowd, where I locked eyes with Theom again. He had a creepy grin on his face, but his eyes seemed normal compared to the last time I saw him. I knew if Theom was around, Rachelle would not be far behind.

"Are you okay?" Opa asked while we picked up the blocks for somebody else to have a turn.

My attention went back to Opa. "I'm okay. I just thought I saw somebody from school," I replied.

"Oh, was it that girl from this morning?" Opa asked.

"No, but how do you know about that?" I asked him.

"Oma filled me in. Don't worry, kiddo. We'll take care of you."

"Thanks, Opa. Can we get some ice cream?"

"Of course!" Opa said and grabbed my hand.

We all walked into the local ice cream parlour. I felt uneasy and kept looking around for Rachelle, expecting to see her at every corner. After a short queue, we got our ice cream and walked out of the store and back onto the main thoroughfare. We took a moment to lick our ice cream cones and talk about what to do next when we were startled by the loud sound of a raven squawking at us from a tree branch. I was not only startled by this occurrence, but almost afraid. Weird that I saw Theom and now a raven only minutes apart—it seemed rather coincidental. I pretended not to see the raven and continued onto the road in the direction of Opa's truck. I saw Opa look back at the tree several times. Had he seen the raven?

We arrived at the truck and opened the doors, and out came a cloud of hot air. We waited for a moment to let the truck cool down before we got in. As we waited, Oma and I ate our ice cream as we watched the crowd. I wondered if I would see Rachelle or Theom again. I wanted to tell Oma about what had happened at the community centre with Theom and the raven, but I hesitated. I needed Opa to tell me where my mom and dad were first before I could trust them. Opa started up the truck, and we got in. The crowd had thinned out since most of the visitors were taking the ferry back to Horseshoe Bay. I wished I was heading back home too. I started to feel homesick again.

As we felt the hum of the truck underneath us, the wind blew through the passenger window. I could smell the grass and the dandelions. I closed my eyes and daydreamed that I was Dorothy on the yellow brick road, walking towards the Emerald City with Olivia, Scarlett, and Alexa behind me.

Then, I realized I had forgotten to buy a cell phone charger. Scarlett, for sure, wouldn't be happy with me not texting her back.

"Oma, is it too late to go back into town to get a cell phone charger?" I asked.

"Most of the shops have closed early because of the festival. Make sure you put it on the grocery list on the kitchen fridge," Oma said.

"Thanks, Oma."

I looked up from the dashboard and noticed a beautiful falcon flying just ahead of us on the road. It was golden in colour, and its wings were spread wide as it glided through the air. It looked like we were following it home.

Oma spoke up, pointing at the falcon. "Jasper, we haven't seen one of those in a while. Mostly eagles around here."

Opa replied, "Yes, very unusual."

We were all quiet as we drove from the paved road onto the dirt road of the driveway to the house. As soon as we got out, the falcon headed towards the Baobab outside my window and circled around it. I suddenly had déjà vu, as I felt like I was reliving my dreams. Something ominous was looming—a feeling that kept being brought up in this ancient place. Oma walked around the passenger side of the truck to go over to Opa.

"Is that who I think it is?" Oma asked.

"I don't know, but I think it's time," Opa said.

Oma looked over at me before she answered, "Yes, Jasper, it's time."

I glared at Opa and Oma, wanting to ask all the questions I had already asked over and over again, but they continued unloading the truck silently. I watched the golden falcon glide above the tree in circles, which was precisely how I felt at this moment. It was like I was running around in circles, trying to figure out what this big secret was and how it may be connected to my dreams. Mostly I needed these answers so I could stop worrying about my mom and dad. Even though I was frustrated, I helped unpack the truck. I was about to go inside but stopped when I saw Opa staring up at the tree. He looked as if he was daydreaming. I grabbed his hand to pull him out of it, and Opa turned to me and smiled.

"Let's clean up and go have dinner," Opa said.

"Yes, I would love that. We're having French toast for dinner! Oma promised!"

"Sounds good to me."

As we prepped the eggs, I still got the feeling that Opa was not with me. *Was he thinking about the falcon? Was it about the big secret he had to tell me?* After inhaling four pieces of French toast, I went to my room. Instantly, Lolo welcomed me by brushing up against my legs and doing circles around both feet. I picked her up and immediately headed to the bedroom window to see if the falcon was still circling the tree, but it was gone. The night seemed strangely quiet. No birds sang. Not even the chirp of crickets could be heard.

I sat down at the desk by the window and looked through the picture book again to see if I recognized anyone familiar, but still, no one stood out. I closed the book and pulled out my drawing pencils and notepad to work on my comic strip. I let out a great big yawn from the long day, feeling drained—both emotionally and physically.

I thought for a moment of my encounters with Rachelle and Theom, and it instantly made me anxious. I also thought of the raven and the falcon. I didn't know what to make of any of it.

5

FRIENDLY CLONES—JULY 2ND, 7:45 AM

It was Monday morning and, unusually, I woke up remembering no dreams from the night before. I got the best night's sleep I had ever had. All that fresh air yesterday at the farmers market was good for me, I guess. It was so early in the morning, but Oma and Opa were already outside working. I knew I needed to be out there with them, so I got dressed, went through the kitchen, grabbed a banana and an apple, and walked out the front door to greet Oma in the garden. As I turned the corner of the house, I felt an energetic pull from the tree outside my bedroom window. The closer I got to the tree, the more I felt it pull me in. It was like electricity running through my hands and down into my feet. I was tingling with this sensation all over.

Lolo was stretched out under the tree having a cat nap, which was odd for her because, at home, she would never want to go outside, even when we left the door or windows open. There was no sign of Opa, so I walked back towards the garden where I saw Oma working.

"Where is Opa?" I asked as I spotted his old, blue Chevy pickup truck in the driveway.

"Opa's out in his workhouse. It's Monday, so it's back to work for him."

"Can I go see what he's doing?" I asked curiously.

"Maybe later. He's too busy fixing shoes for his customers. I think it would be best to stay away. He gets agitated when I try to go in and clean up his shop."

Oma came closer to me and said in a hushed voice, "You know, Opa was a very famous shoemaker in his day. He used to make shoes for European royals! He also has a collection of extraordinary shoes that maybe you'll get to see soon." Oma looked around as she mentioned this unique shoe collection, as if she wanted to make sure there wasn't anyone around to overhear us. I wasn't sure what could be so special about a shoe collection, but I went along with it.

"Oh, Mom and Dad never told me that! Is today the day I get to find out what happened to them and what the big family secret is?" I asked slyly, or so I thought, sneaking in my real question.

"Opa will tell you all about it, but right now, we're both busy working."

Getting frustrated with the stalling, I decided to initiate my Plan B: if they wouldn't tell me, then I would find out for myself.

At that moment, I knew what I needed to do to get started on my plan.

"Oma, I'm heading back inside to get my hat. It's hot out here."

"Okay, Bella, don't be too long. I could use your help in digging up these weeds."

"No problem, Oma," I said, eager to get going on my adventure. I ran through the house and upstairs to my room. I pulled out an old, gray, brimmed hat from my luggage, and when I set it on my head, I took a moment to look at the suitcase. My dad had given it to me. It was his once. I stopped myself from remembering simpler times when my family was near and safe. I shook myself of the nostalgia and put on a determined face. It was time for me to be a detective and look for some clues. I decided that whenever I had a moment between chores, I would run inside and go through each room of the house.

Today I would focus on the study. As I walked in, I was immediately reminded of a museum. It was covered in dark wood and big leather chairs, and it had a large, old desk. I eyed the desk, thinking it would be an excellent place to start. On top of the desk was a photo album full of pictures of Opa when he was younger, but there was nothing unusual about that, so I set it aside and started sifting through loose papers and folders. One folder I found contained information about time travel, which sounded cool but strange. The folder also contained an old Egyptian story of a woman named Rhodopis, which seemed to have been ripped out of a book. *Who was she, and why was this story here on the desk?*

I read through it, fascinated by the tale.

Rhodopis was a young woman who was captured in Greece and sold as a slave in Egypt. The man that bought her was kind and treated her well, but the other slaves in his house did not. They teased her for looking different from them, so her only friends were animals, and she took excellent care of her animal friends. She would give them her extra food, and she would play with them. Sometimes she would even sing and dance for them.

One evening, her master saw her performing for the animals, and he decided that anyone who could dance as beautifully as she deserved some lovely shoes to dance in, so he bought her a special pair of red slippers. These slippers were so beautiful it was thought that the gods themselves had made them.

A little while after this, there was word that the king of Egypt would hold a ball, and he invited the entire kingdom to participate. All of Rhodopis's house was invited, but as they put on their finest clothes to go to the celebration, the other slaves piled Rhodopis with all of their unfinished chores and left without her. Rhodopis was so sad and hurt, she sang lamenting songs as she washed clothes by the river, watching the others pole away on their raft towards the ball. Her songs were overheard by a falcon who swooped down and snatched up one of her shoes that was left on the bank of the river. Rhodopis clutched the other shoe to her breast and cried mightily, as she had never felt so defeated before in her life.

While at the ball, the Pharaoh watched as the rest of the kingdom enjoyed the party, but he could only feel boredom. As he sat in his throne watching the celebration before him, a red slipper was dropped in his lap by a falcon. He knew the falcon to be the god, Horus. The gods were telling him that the owner of this shoe would become his wife, so he set out immediately to find who it belonged to.

He travelled the kingdom far and wide to find the owner of the slipper, but no one could fit in such a dainty shoe. Finally, he arrived at the home of Rhodopis, but she was so frightened by the horns and the carriages of the Pharaoh's entourage that she hid behind some rushes by the river, away from the commotion. The other slaves in the household tried on the slipper and pretended it fit, although it was very clear that their feet were far too large. As the Pharaoh was about to leave the house, he spotted Rhodopis's hiding place and asked her to come forward to try on the shoe. To everyone's amazement, the slipper fit her perfectly, so she then pulled out the matching slipper she had saved. The Pharaoh then knew he had found his wife. The other slaves complained that she wasn't Egyptian enough to rule Egypt, but the Pharaoh said she was the most Egyptian of all: her eyes were green like the Nile, her hair golden like the papyrus, and her skin pink like the lotus.

I put the story down and evaluated what I had just read. I couldn't help but feel sad for Rhodopis's suffering, but also happy that her story ended so wonderfully. Her story reminded me of a lot of Cinderella. I wondered if Horus, the golden falcon in the Rhodopis story, was related to the falcon in my dreams. I suddenly thought of Scarlett. I could hear her laughing at me and my overactive imagination. *Wow, I must be going crazy.*

I heard Opa calling for me, his voice ripping through the hundreds of thoughts racing through my head. "Orabella, where are you?"

I quickly put everything back, hoping it was the way I found it. *Was the photo album on top? Or was it the folder of time travelling papers?* I could hear Opa's footsteps coming nearer. I shuffled things around a bit more, hoping that the mess would be distraction enough, and I walked out of the study casually.

Opa was there in the hallway looking at me. "What are you doing, Bella?"

"I was looking for a piece of paper to doodle on," I replied nonchalantly. I felt guilty for lying, but if he wasn't telling me the truth, then I didn't have to tell him the truth either.

"Well, you need to help your Oma with the weeds. She's been out there a while waiting for you."

Shoot! I had forgotten entirely about my chores! "Right, right, Opa, I was just heading outside!" I smiled and skipped past him, feeling sly and accomplished.

The day passed by with lots of chores to do, but I never got a chance to go back inside and look around again. Opa and Oma always seemed to be waiting for me in the house somewhere. *Did they suspect my snooping?*

I was outside watering some of the plants when Opa came out of his shed and called out to me.

"We need to start putting things away. There's a storm coming."

I looked up and saw the dark clouds gathering in the sky and saw the branches of the Baobab swinging in the wind that had picked up. I put down my hose and started clearing all of the tools we had used during the day.

Opa called out again, "We need to close all the windows in the house!"

"Okay, Opa!" I set my things aside and ran to the front door, where I ran into Oma. "Storm's coming!" I said hastily. Oma rushed past me outside to put the chickens away, and I started going through the whole house, closing all the windows.

Soon Opa and Oma met me inside, and we all made dinner. We were quiet while we ate, but the wind outside kept blowing and howling. It felt like it was pushing against the house. Oma got up from the dinner table to get some candles just in case the lights went out. Sure enough, a few minutes later, the whole house was completely dark.

We all got ready for bed using our flashlights. The house creaked and moaned, and as I lay in bed with Lolo beside me, I realized it was another day without answers. *Will they ever tell me the truth?*

I looked up at the ceiling and saw the tree's shadow dancing across it. Mesmerized by the twisting shadow branches, I felt myself slip off into a dream, fading into another world.

In the dream, I saw myself sneaking around a dark attic. I felt like there was someone in there with me, but whenever I pointed my flashlight to see what lurked in the corners, there was nothing there. I felt my heart pounding in my chest. I spotted a trunk in the back corner of the small room. The ceiling was low, so I bent my head down as I crept over to it. On top of the piece of old luggage was a newspaper clipping. The article was in a foreign language, but the picture that accompanied the story was of my Opa. He was young, maybe 20 years old, and he was putting a shoe on a woman who looked to be a princess or a queen, for she had a delicate tiara woven into her hair.

I was elated at the discovery of my Opa's fame, but while I studied the article, trying to make out any words that I could, my heart nearly leapt out of my throat when a mouse scampered across my foot. I yelped and jumped backwards but quickly put my hand over my mouth so Opa and Oma would not hear me. I put the newspaper clipping down next to the old trunk so I could open the lid to look inside. It was easy to open despite its age, like it had been used recently. Inside the trunk was only a small, bulging pouch that I grabbed and pulled open to take a look inside. The fabric of the pouch unfolded in my palm to reveal a key. The key was golden in colour and had a spiral at the top with a green emerald. As I touched the spiral with my fingers, my vision blurred, and I felt myself falling inwards, as if my eyes could now only watch my dreams instead of the world around me. The key was drawing me in. A sense of calm came over me, and all I wanted to do was sleep.

Off in the distance, I heard Oma's voice calling to me. My attention snapped back to the present, and I quickly pulled my eyes away from the key and ran quietly to the attic door. I looked back at the trunk that I had left open knowing I needed to close it and return the key, but I could hear Oma's footsteps drawing near the stairs of the attic. It was too late. I shoved the key in my pocket.

I bounced down the stairs as Oma was on her way up.

"Orabella, what are you up to?" she asked.

"Oh, just chilling."

She had a puzzled look on her face and replied, "The chickens need to be fed, and the backyard needs to be raked. We must keep up with things. We're starting to enter fall."

Fall? How did that happen? I ran to the door and looked out at the yard. There was a sprinkle of leaves on the ground, but the air still felt warm. I walked outside to do the chores like Oma asked, but I kept getting distracted with the chickens. When I finally finished, I spent the rest of the afternoon under the Baobab daydreaming.

I felt so relaxed, but there was a voice in my head that kept nagging at me that time was slipping away from me. I tried to ignore it because I didn't want to leave the tree.

Nothing else in the world mattered at that moment besides the tree.

I thought that sometimes I stared at it for too long, because I started seeing lights floating around the branches and the trunk, but then I'd blink a couple of times and the lights would go away. I held my focus on the branches, and again lights drifted in and out of my sight, cascading down from the leaves like snowflakes in the wintertime. I felt their warmth as they brushed my cheeks, smiling with each soft caress.

Without warning, I was suddenly back in my bed.

How did I get here? A moment ago, it was daytime, and I was outside, and now it's nighttime, and I'm in bed. Where is Lolo? Am I still dreaming?

I felt my reasoning muddle as another dream started taking over my consciousness. I could see very clearly the outline of a door in the trunk of the Baobab. I took the key out of my pocket and fit it in the keyhole. I turned it, but nothing happened. I turned it again and heard a roar beneath me, as if the whole Earth was shaking and colliding, but nothing around me moved. The Earth remained still even though the sound rumbled on.

Then, the wooden door of the tree opened with a loud, creaking wail. As it slowly opened inward, a golden light started to burst through. I hesitated to walk in at first, but the light called to me the same way the tree had with an electric sensation, a tingling, a pleasant warmness. I walked forward and saw a spiral, golden stairway leading downwards. As I walked to the top of the stairs, I could smell fresh flowers. The smell seemed to be wafting up from the bottom of the stairwell.

I slowly descended the stairs, the smell of flowers ripening with each step. When I got to the bottom, a gaping mouth to a tunnel opened before me, and beyond it, a brighter golden light. I kept walking towards the light, through the entrance of the tunnel, following the light ahead of me into an oval-shaped room full of shoes, almost like a library of shoes.

There were thousands of cubbies surrounding the walls of the room, each one containing a different pair of shoes. Many looked very old-fashioned and multicultural. Each one was perfect in shape and colour like they were new, or as if time had stood still for them. As I walked around the room, looking into each cubby, a card was displayed with the shoes that told the history of each pair. The room somehow felt big and small at the same time, and in the middle of it stood an old stone desk with what looked like a dark green book also made of stone on top of it. Decorating the cover of the book was an oval stone, embellished with golden spirals, and beside it was an emerald necklace the same colour as the book.

As I walked closer to the desk, I noticed a newspaper with a red circle around an ad:

"WANTED: Somebody to go back in time. This is not a joke. P.O. BOX 0427 2949 Main Street, Vancouver BC, V5T-5S4. You will get paid after we get back. Must bring your own weapon. Safety is not guaranteed. I have done this several times. Need to save a friend."

What a weird ad. But the P.O. box number looked familiar: 0427. *I know that number.* I looked up from the desk and noticed there were two antique chairs in the far corners of the room, and somebody was sitting in each of them.

Both were shadows. The shadow to the left was more massive and felt sinister, and the shadow to the right was slightly smaller and less threatening. I got goosebumps all over me. I squinted my eyes to see if I could make out who they were, but all I could see were blurry figures of darkness.

The one on my right said, "Welcome home," which made me feel reassured and safe, but then the one on the left spoke. "We finally found you."

My hair stood on end; it was the same voice I had heard in my head the night of the Summer Solstice Festival.

I woke with a start in my bed and looked around in confusion. It seemed like mid-morning, as the sun was bright outside. I wished I had a clock to know what the exact time was. Then I heard knocking on my door, and I jumped out of bed.

"Orabella, we have visitors downstairs," Oma said brightly from behind the closed door.

"Coming!" I called out as I sat on the edge of the bed and tried to wake up fully. *Wow, did I just have a dream within a dream? That was so freaky.* I thought about the key and looked under my pillow, wondering if it had been a dream or real life. There was nothing there.

For as long as I could remember, I had always dreamt of the falcon and the tree, but something about being at Oma and Opa's was giving me crazy dreams about all sorts of things. I laughed at how wild my imagination had become and picked some clothes out of my suitcase to wear for the day. I got dressed and felt my excitement grow in anticipation of finally learning the truth about myself. I walked downstairs and into the kitchen and saw two girls sitting at the table talking with Oma.

As I approached the kitchen, they both turned around, and I stared directly into the eyes of my friends, Scarlett and Georgia. My jaw dropped. I looked at my friends, but it was not them. Something felt off—their eyes were different. There were flickers of green in them, and I knew that both Scarlett and Georgia had brown eyes.

They introduced themselves. The first was Georgia. She looked like she always had: tall and thin with long black hair. She had the body of a gymnast or a ballerina. But this Georgia had a thick, Chinese accent. I stared into her strange and unfamiliar eyes. *It is Georgia, but not the Georgia I know.*

The other girl had dark hair, big soft eyes, and she too had an accent—a Spanish accent. I was confused about why they were here, and I wondered if they were clones of my friends or something else entirely. The girls seemed nice, but it was unsettling to have them here at the breakfast table. Where were their parents?

Oma spoke up to break the silence. "Opa and I thought it would be best if you had a little homeschooling while you were here. The girls are here to teach you about their different cultures. Georgia will be teaching you to speak Mandarin, and Scarlett will be teaching you Spanish."

I was not thrilled about this. Oma sounded so excited, but I just felt overwhelmed. I kept staring and wondering how they could look just like my friends yet not be them. It was hard for me to tear my gaze from their eyes—something about them was mesmerizing.

Then, it hit me. I hadn't had time to think about where I would be going to school. The chores, the slower way of life, and the odd dreams had preoccupied my time. I got angry at Oma as neither she nor Opa had told me about my mom or dad yet. My life had changed dramatically without my knowledge or approval.

"What about my mom and dad? When are you going to tell me the truth? School is not important right now. I need to know where they are!" I demanded as I held back tears.

As the two girls stood in front of me, blankness in their eyes, overwhelming feelings bubbled up inside. There was a ringing in my ears. I wanted to run out of the room, but I was frozen in place, desperately trying to hold myself together. My body began to shake. Small, at first, but then giant waves overtook me until I felt myself pushing past everyone in the kitchen to race out of the house and through the backyard, my legs moving like they never had before. I was running, but where to? As I ran, I kept pushing myself to go faster to outrun the anger and fear.

I ran from the house onto the road. I could hear Oma yelling out to me, but all I could do at that moment was keep running. I ran till the road became a dirt path that ended at the beach. I wanted to jump in and swim as far as I could. Instead, I collapsed onto the sand and cried until my eyes stung.

I sat looking out at the ocean, sad and confused. I wanted to cry more but couldn't. I was exhausted and empty. I looked down at myself, and I was completely covered in sand. I was so lost in thought that the day flew by. The sun shifted from behind me to the front of me, and I sat there in a daze for hours until I felt a hand rest on my shoulder. I jumped at the touch, not expecting anyone to find me here. The hand belonged to Opa. I had forgotten how tall he was, even taller than Dad. His deep blue eyes and wrinkled forehead stared down at me kindly.

"Orabella, may I sit beside you?"

Opa reminded me of my dad, sensitive and warm. He sat down beside me on the sand. "You ran off so quickly that it was hard to track you down. Took all day to find you," he said.

I looked at him apologetically, but all of my energy had been sapped from me. I didn't want to play this game anymore.

"Orabella, why did you run from the house?"

"I was scared and angry. I feared those girls because they looked weird to me. They looked just like my friends, but their eyes were strange. And, because neither you nor Oma has said anything about my parents' disappearance. I've been waiting for an answer, but you've both avoided telling me what happened."

"Orabella, Oma thought that it would be best to introduce you to the truth by educating you over the summer with the girls. But I see now how much this is affecting you, and Oma and I agree that it's time for you to know."

"Okay, Opa. May I tell you something first?"

He nodded his head. "Of course."

"Opa, I need to tell you that, for as long as I can remember, I've had dreams about moving here. Like everything I've ever done has brought me to your home. But being here, it doesn't feel the way I thought it would. I feel scared. I feel confused. I miss my mom and dad.

"In my dreams, I have a purpose: I'm following a golden falcon to a magical tree—a tree that looks just like the Baobab in the yard!" I looked to Opa for a reaction, but he remained silent. I decided to press on and tell him more details.

"Then the golden falcon who circles the tree is suddenly flying out of an orange sun. It lands on a branch across the river, directly in front of me. The falcon is staring at me, and the wind picks up and blows in all directions. The falcon starts to speak to me in my head. It says, 'Welcome home,' which relates to another dream I had where I heard those words, but we can talk about that later." I could feel myself rambling, but Opa looked like he was still following along.

"Then, in the dream, the golden falcon asks me the question, 'Does a person choose the journey or does the journey choose the person?'

"I say to the falcon, 'Trust your destiny, have faith, and give in.'

"Then, I wake up! But it feels like this dream becomes clearer after each birthday," I explained. "Every year, the dream develops into a clearer message."

Opa looked at me. "That is really quite the dream. It appears that the gods have been trying to tell you about your destiny for a long time."

I looked at him blankly, waiting for more of an explanation.

"Come, let's go." Opa began walking to the truck. Even though he said very little, I knew the time had come for me to learn about everything. My head was swirling. I was finally going to know the truth.

I had to break the silence. "Opa, why did the girls at the house look like my friends back in the city? It was so weird, especially their eyes!"

"Those girls are here to help you prepare for something, but we must start at the beginning. You must be patient a little while longer."

I decided to switch subjects to get my mind off it all. "What was my dad like growing up? Was Dad like me?"

Opa laughed. "Not as stubborn as you, but he was adventurous and a seeker very much like yourself."

I blushed. "What do you mean?"

"Oh, I've noticed you sneaking around the house. I was a little worried you were going to try to sneak into my workshop before the time was right to tell you everything."

"What's in the workshop? Is that where the big secret is? Are my mom and dad hiding there?"

There were no answers to these questions. We were both quiet as we arrived at the truck.

Opa opened up the truck door for me, which again reminded me of his kindness and sincerity. Then Opa started the truck, put it into gear, and pulled out from the parking lot and back on to the road home.

"Why is it so hard for you to tell me what is going on?" I asked Opa as the summer wind blew through the truck cabin.

Opa changed gears in the truck. "There is so much to tell you. To be honest, I don't know where to begin, and I don't want to make the same mistakes I made with your dad. We've never quite agreed on what to tell you."

"Tell me what? What mistake are you talking about? Is that why you and Dad aren't talking to each other?"

"We have a long history of disagreeing. I lost my son, and I didn't want to lose you too, so I was looking for the perfect time to tell you," Opa replied.

As we drove into the driveway, Oma stood close to the mailbox, waiting for us. "Where did you run to? I was so worried."

"She ran down to the beach," Opa replied.

Oma laughed. "That's where your father would go as a child. He spent a lot of time there. Your dad was a loner, always carrying the weight of the world on his shoulders," Oma said in a sad voice.

"Orabella, give me a moment with Oma. Then we can go to the workshop."

Opa and Oma walked away from me and stood close to the house. They were surely arguing about my stunt, but both grandparents turned and smiled at me, reassuring me they weren't mad.

"We both feel you are ready to know the truth about your destiny," Opa told me.

Seriously? Destiny?

How could they know about my destiny, considering I felt my life here was temporary, and destiny seemed so permanent? How was that possible when life was so unpredictable? I felt like I was about to cry again.

As we walked towards the house, Opa and I split off from Oma and started walking towards Opa's workshop. I was scared and excited at the same time. I suddenly turned back towards Oma, knowing that things were going to change. I was not sure how, but life would be different from now on. Oma looked at me and said mysteriously, "Safe journey, Orabella."

6

CLUELESS CLUES—JULY 2ND, 8:45 PM

Oma's words rang hard in my head as another level of confusion rose, yet another part of me felt the mystery of being here would uncover itself soon enough. We walked towards the workshop, which was off to the right of the driveway and the main house. It was shaped like a small, blue barn, more worn than the main house, with its white paint chipping off the sides. When we entered Opa's workspace, I was immediately taken by its worn-in feeling and busy messiness. There were tools and shoes everywhere.

I looked around at the pictures that covered the walls: old posters of Holland and photos of Oma, Mom, Dad, Auntie, and me. All over the shop were shoe machines and shoes that were being repaired or mended. Opa had walked to the back of the space to an unremarkable brown door, where he motioned at me to join him. I gingerly walked towards him, trying not to knock over any of his work on my way.

He opened the door, which revealed an old metal staircase that spiralled down into a basement. As I grabbed onto the smooth, metal railing, I had a strong feeling of déjà vu, like I had walked down these stairs before. The stairwell was so different from the dusty shoe shop; it was clean—stark, uncluttered. When we got to the bottom of the stairs, there was a large wooden door with symbols carved into the frame. I stared at the symbols for a moment but didn't recognize them as any language that I knew. Opa then pushed it open, which led to another room. My dream came flooding back to me. This room was exactly as I remembered. The shoes, the cards, and a book made of green stone. *Was my dream even a dream at all?*

Opa studied my face as I took in the room and asked, "You've dreamt about this room, haven't you?"

I nodded my head, too excited to speak. To my right were two big brown leather chairs and a wooden pedestal that held the book on it. I went around the whole room, looking and touching. There was a low ringing in my ears, and I felt a tingling sensation throughout my body. I reached out to touch the strange, green book, which had a beautiful necklace beside it that looked to be made of the same stone. It was as if someone had carved an oval out of the book and put it on a chain to be worn.

"Orabella, please don't touch the Book until I've told you everything. Here, let's sit down." Opa motioned to the leather chairs.

"Opa, how did you know I had a dream about this room?" I asked curiously.

"Orabella, dreams for us are messages—much like your dream of the falcon—and sometimes our dreams can prepare us for future events."

"Like a fortune-teller?"

"In a way, but let me start from the beginning. You'll understand once I tell you everything."

I set my mouth tight, trying to listen rather than talk even though my mind was racing a million kilometres an hour. I looked at my grandfather expectantly.

"My father sat with me here, and I sat here with your father. I'm going to tell you the same stories, which will help you understand your path. These are myths and legends that will give you a greater understanding of your destiny.

"This is not just about you, but your entire lineage: your dad, me, your great-grandfather, and everyone that came before us."

"Like a family curse or something?" I couldn't help but let that slip out.

Opa shot me a glance that told me to pipe down, but he still patiently answered my question. "For some of us, it has felt that way.

"There are many stories that I will tell you, each one separated in history and context, but they'll eventually weave together to reveal the bigger picture."

Opa scooted back in his chair and cleared his throat. Then, he began, "At the beginning of time, there was the creator god named Amun-Ra, and this all-powerful being created everything in the world: right and wrong, justice and power, the rain and the sun . . . everything. Two of his first creations were the Eye of Ra and the Eye of Horus.

The right eye was the Eye of Horus, which represented the moon. The left eye, the Eye of Ra, represented the sun, and the sun was protected by the goddess Wadjet. The two eyes are contrasting entities, like light and dark, and without one, you cannot have the other."

Opa continued, "So Horus and Wadjet were in charge of quite a lot, being that they were the sun and the moon. But a great part of their responsibilities was to protect all of Ancient Egypt—its people and its rulers. Do you know the story of Rhodopis and how she came to rule Egypt?"

"Yes, I read the article in your study," I said abashedly.

Opa gave me a little glare but moved on without reprimanding me. "Well, after Horus dropped Rhodopis's slipper into the Pharaoh's lap, the two were married by Horus himself. And as a gift to them, he granted their newborn son special abilities to protect the world and its inhabitants, much like Horus and Wadjet did for Egypt. The Pharaoh's son would be known as the first Soljourner, and every male descendant thereafter would also be a Soljourner. Soljourners are the protectors of the Tree of Life, maintaining the balance of knowledge and creativity, and maintaining the balance of good and evil."

"Okay, Opa, but how does this relate to everything that's been going on?" I asked impatiently.

"It is your destiny to be a Soljourner, just as your father was—just as I was. We are descendants of the Pharaoh and Rhodopis, and we are guardians of the Tree of Life."

My jaw dropped open. I would have laughed had I not been in such disbelief.

"But I'm a girl. You said that it was only the males that would be Soljourners."

"According to a prophecy written by Horus, after the first Soljourner, only boys would be born to protect the Tree, but when a girl Soljourner was born, she would be the last of our kind. Orabella, you are the last Soljourner."

7

DESTINY—JULY 2ND, 9:45 PM

I blinked my eyes at Opa, trying to soak in all of this information. "Okay, so I'm a protector of the Tree of Life. What exactly is the Tree of Life? I mean, I remember Oma saying something about it, but why does it need to be protected?"

"The Tree of Life is the energy of the Earth that connects all living things. It connects humans to nature, it connects humans to animals, and it connects humans to each other. The Tree of Life grows out of the spirit of the Earth and its inhabitants. It grows through art, inspiration, creativity, and expression, and its branches thread through the hearts of all living beings. The Tree of Life thrives when humans feed it with their inventions and ingenuity. Even love feeds the Tree, but some beings exist in the world that would prefer to see the Tree die. This is where we come in as Soljourners. We must prevent the Tree from being damaged."

"What? Why? The world would be a terrible place if we didn't have art or music or love!" I interjected.

"Well, there are some beings that don't live in the same realm as us. They don't live as we do; they don't find joy as we do."

"There are different realms?"

"Well, think of the world as a large apartment building with many floors as far as you can see. Now, let's say that each floor is a dimension, and humanity is on one floor, and you live in one of these apartments. There are billions of apartments on your floor, but each apartment is a separate reality. Some people come into your life, like me, your parents, and even your friends—it's like we are visiting your apartment. It would be nearly impossible to visit every single apartment, but just because you don't go into every single one, that doesn't mean those realities don't exist.

"But there are also floors below and above our own, and these other floors are apartments too, but they are homes for beings that most of us think are just fairy tales, like angels, demons, gods and goddesses—and everything else that humans' imaginations have created."

"Whoa, Opa. You're telling me they're real?" I raised my voice in wonder.

"Very much so," Opa replied seriously.

I knitted my eyebrows together in thought. There was so much to know. Maybe I would get to meet a fairy one day! *Focus, focus . . .*

Opa spoke before I could come up with a new question to ask. "There are times when humans invite these other beings to our floor. There are also a select few of us who can visit the other floors, and this is when the Tree becomes endangered, because not everyone treats the Tree with the same amount of respect. Some would deplete the Tree of its nutrients for their benefit. They upset the balance that keeps the Tree healthy."

I gave Opa a puzzled look.

Opa saw my face and explained, "For living things to survive, they need to be fed."

"Yes, just like when Oma and I water the plants and feed the chickens."

"Exactly! That is why we ask you to do these chores, so you understand the responsibility of taking care of others. If you don't feed a living thing, it will die."

"Yes, that makes sense," I said, "but then why do some of the apartments not want to feed the Tree? Wouldn't that affect them too if the Tree died?"

"Very perceptive. Well, since some of these beings don't require the same conditions to live as we do, such as oxygen, food, nature, love, and art, they do not care about the health of the Tree. They only care about sustaining themselves. And these creatures that are focused solely on themselves thrive off of the pain that they provide others. They are fueled by chaos, anger, and hatred, and they feed off the creatures of that floor instead of helping to feed the Tree.

"Because of this, the Tree's health is compromised. Its balance is tipped, and the beings that would prefer discord outweigh the beings that would see the Tree thrive. The Tree becomes weak if the darkness prevails and not enough of the light shines through. As humans, we are pivotal in maintaining the health of the Tree because we are the only beings in the universe that are graced with free will. We can choose to be light or dark, whereas the other dimensions do not have that same luxury. They are born into the darkness or born into the light. Because of our free will, we can choose how we respond to actions and situations."

"Just like the story of the white wolf and the black wolf," I interjected.

"Yes, Oma loves that tale. Every human has these two sides to them. It is up to us to decide which one gains more strength than the other."

"Okay, Opa, but if all humans can help the Tree of Life, why were the Soljourners created?"

"Good question. Remember how Horus and Wadjet were responsible for protecting Ancient Egypt?"

I nodded my head vigorously.

"Well, the day came that Rhodopis and the Pharaoh were directly subjected to the wrath of the darkness. They went missing, stolen in the night, and Horus and Wadjet knew they could not fight the darkness alone. They needed a human to aid them in their battle to maintain the balance and the health of the Tree. So, they enlisted the help of the Pharaoh's son, and they trained him to fight the beings that would see the Tree destroyed.

"Though there are many creatures that bolster the darkness, there is one that has risen above the others as a leader. His name is Iblis. Iblis went after the Pharaoh and Rhodopis to cripple the power of Horus and to injure humanity and the Tree of Life."

"Is this what happened to my mom and dad? Did Iblis kidnap them? How do we save them? How do we get them back?"

Even with all of this information, I still felt that there were so many unanswered questions. I could sense that my heart wanted to race and panic, but somehow my brain was able to remain calm. I felt a sense of pride in that. I was learning. I was growing.

"I don't know. I've used the Emerald Stone to help track them both, but it's like they've disappeared from existence altogether. I fear I don't have any answers for you about where they've gone or who took them." Opa looked down, defeated.

"What is the Emerald Stone?"

Opa looked up again with more confidence this time, knowing he could answer the question. "It is this necklace here." Opa walked over to the pedestal and held up the green necklace. "For the Pharaoh's son to be successful in helping Horus and Wadjet, he needed to learn everything that they already knew. And that was a huge amount of information, as Horus and Wadjet existed from the very beginning of time—they were the sun and the moon; they could see every moment that had ever been created. No human would ever be able to contain as much information as they knew, so the gods created a book within which their information would be stored for the Soljourners to learn from, and the Emerald Stone is what helps us retain what we've read from the Book."

I stood up and followed him. When I looked at the book, it was both opaque and transparent at the same time, as if the light was trapped within it rather than being reflected off of it. The only adornment on the cover was a raised oval in the very centre that had golden spirals attaching it to the cover. I wanted to reach out and touch it, but I kept my hands to myself, knowing Opa had already told me once not to touch it.

Opa began speaking again, running a finger along with the book. "This is the Emerald Book. Wadjet travelled the cosmos in search of a material that could contain such powerful knowledge. After searching the Earth and the universe, it wasn't until she happened upon a black hole that she was rewarded in her quest. When Wadjet entered the black hole, she was taken to the centre of the universe. There stood two trees: one above and one below—perfect mirrors of each other. These were the Trees of Existence: the Tree of Life and the Tree of Knowledge.

"She introduced herself to the Trees as the energy that held the world together. In response to Wadjet, a single piece of green crystal formed in front of her. It was the Trees' gift to her. It was the material she required to hold all the information of life. And it is this Emerald Book that is before us."

I stared at the book, imagining the information held within. *I can't wait to read it!*

"Opa, why do you have the stone and the Book and not Dad? Are these things not passed on as you say?"

"Yes, they are, but your father chose to walk a different path. He felt he found a better way, saying that the Soljourners have been failures. We have continued with these missions and have followed these ways without success. I tried to explain to him that it is not about winning or losing, but about maintaining the balance. But he didn't see it that way. We're not out to destroy the darkness. We've fought many times over our family's role as protectors of the Tree of Life, but those fights only led to him rejecting me and rejecting his title as a Soljourner. The last time we saw each other, he left me with the necklace. He has not had its protection for some time now."

"Do you think Dad got himself into trouble?"

"I don't know. We haven't spoken in years. Marcus didn't want help and didn't want to use any of the tools that were passed on to him."

"But if he didn't have the stone or Book, then how did he travel back in time like in that photo next to the car?"

"He used to, but after his first mission, your dad came back changed. I'm not sure what happened, but he chose to walk away from this—from us."

As Opa trailed off, I tried to process all that had been told to me. My thoughts were racing through my head. It was hard for me to believe this to be true, but a part of me already knew it was. I felt this tug of war within me. I just wanted to be a kid, but to accept my destiny and this responsibility would mean I could never be a kid again. I knew it was my duty to be this protector that Opa was telling me I was, but I could barely protect myself from a single bully at school! How was I going to protect the entire human race?

Opa chuckled lightly. "Perhaps one day, they will be telling the myth and legend of the famous Orabella."

I stood up and dramatically made a heroic pose and bounced back into the oversized chair. I was so eager to hear more, yet there was already so much information to grasp.

"Opa, quickly, before you begin another story, I need to go to the bathroom."

Opa laughed. "It's back upstairs in the work shed."

I climbed up the spiral staircase and back onto the main floor into the bathroom. In the mirror, I saw my brown eyes flash green. I did a double-take and got closer to the mirror to look at my eyes, but they appeared normal. I suddenly shivered and remembered I had to go to the bathroom. *It was just a light reflecting in the mirror.*

I came back down the stairs, settled back into the oversized, brown leather chair, and looked over at Opa. He had his eyes closed, but when he opened them, I saw his crystal blue eyes flash green. I stared into his eyes to make sure of what I had seen, but it was gone as quickly as it had come.

"Opa, I keep seeing a green flash in my eyes. Yours too. Even with those two girls that came over. What is that?" I asked.

Opa pointed back to the green book on the wooden pedestal.

"Cool," I said, sinking back into my chair, waiting for Opa to share more stories. I quickly glanced at the clock on the wall and saw it was 11:30 PM. I could not believe three hours had already passed!

"Let's go outside for a walk. It will help keep our minds fresh. Maybe we can walk along the creek," Opa suggested.

8

RAVEN'S RETURN—JULY 2ND, 8:30 PM

As we walked towards the creek, the colours of the sky glowed bright orange, blue, and purple. It was sunset, but that seemed impossible, as the sun was on the horizon when we first got back from the beach.

"Opa, why does it feel like time has gone backwards now that we're outside?"

"Ah, I guess I forgot to mention that time slows down for us whenever we are around the Emerald Book. We could spend days downstairs, but life would be almost frozen all around us. That's why you will do most of your training down there."

"So, we could spend a year down there learning and come up here, and only a few weeks will have gone by?"

"Yes, you will be able to gain quite a lot of knowledge in a short period of time. The only exception is when you go location scouting. That will happen on Earth's time because you'll have to become familiar with the area you will be travelling to," Opa replied with a smile.

I stayed quiet as we continued to walk along the property, the warm summer wind rustling through the trees. The temperature was warm but not unpleasant, and the frogs started calling to each other along the creek as they always did at twilight. Everything was so peaceful until the caw of a raven ripped through the evening air. I whirled around to see that it was sitting on one of the branches of the Baobab. It continued to caw as it jumped from branch to branch like it was following us. Opa turned around to look at it, but it was gone. We continued on our walk.

The smell of the creek reminded me of the fishing trips I used to go on with my dad. Lolo appeared by the side of a tree with an annoyed look on her face. I guess I hadn't given her enough attention today. She made a beeline for me and jumped into my arms, snuggling into me.

"I see your little protector is here."

"Yes, she is. She's always here for me. Lolo is not like any normal cat. It's like she's human in some ways," I told him.

Opa continued to grin. Lolo looked up, and I could see a glint of green in her eyes, which I hadn't noticed before. I suddenly grabbed her and hugged her, feeling overcome with affection. "I love you, my little Lolo."

"Lolo is no ordinary cat. She's here to protect you."

Lolo is my protector? I somehow was not as surprised by that information as I thought I would be.

"I think that's a good enough walk. We've had enough fresh air for us to keep going. Let's head back to the workplace," Opa said.

I held Lolo in my arms as we began the descent into what I now called the Shoe Chamber. As I followed Opa into the room, I paused in my steps when I saw a raven sitting on top of the wooden pedestal where the Book resided. I turned to Opa, alarmed, and pointed my finger at it.

Opa stepped in front of me as if to protect me from the bird.

"How did a raven get in here?" I asked.

"This is no ordinary raven," he said and slowly walked towards it.

"Is that the same raven we saw at the creek just now?

"I think it must be. Hello, Morrigan. It's been a while," Opa spoke to the bird.

Suddenly, a cold breeze ran through the room. Lolo started hissing immediately and jumped out of my arms. I stepped back in surprise at Lolo's reaction, but when I looked up, I watched the raven shake its feathers with a motion so powerful, it seemed to be pushing the air molecules apart from each other. The bird and the air shook again, and before us stood a woman where the raven once was. She was taller than Opa and slender, with long black hair down to her pointy hips. Her shiny black eyes had no whites to them. Her lips were black, and her skin was pale. She was beautiful, but her dark eyes stared through me with the most sinister of intentions.

"Yes, it has been a while. I guess you have not been near death for some time."

"Opa, who is this?" I asked, trying to be heard over Lolo's hissing.

"Orabella, I would like you to meet Morrigan. She is the goddess of life and death. She helps move souls through cycles, from life to death, and from death to life."

"Whoa, I know of her, but why is she here?" I asked nervously.

"Hello, little one, I'm so happy to finally meet you, considering you have been so well-protected," Morrigan spoke with a deep voice as she stared at Lolo.

Lolo's hissing got louder.

"Yes, Morrigan, why are you here? Normally you're only around when death is near," Opa said with a scowl.

"I am. I smell it all around you." She paused before continuing. "But I also wanted to come and introduce myself to the young and powerful one here. She honoured me by dressing up like me for her little festival."

Opa looked at me, confused as to why I would dress up like Morrigan. Then, he looked at her with his eyes squinted in skepticism. "Morrigan, what is it you really want?" Opa asked.

I stood behind Opa, and I could see him clutch the stone necklace tightly in his hand behind his back. Lolo was still hissing like crazy.

"Jasper, the little one is so precious, and if she is to ever need my help, she could always call out to me," Morrigan informed him innocently.

"Morrigan, we both know that if she ever did that, then she would owe you something in return. We can't have that."

Morrigan moved closer to Opa. It was then that I noticed she hadn't walked over to him but had floated above the floor.

"Well, I sensed death, and perhaps it is because you are about to talk about Iblis," Morrigan replied.

"Have you been listening to what I have been telling Orabella? How is that possible under the protection of the Tree and the Book?" Opa asked, surprised.

"When I smell death, nothing can keep me from it, Jasper. You know this. So, can I say 'hello' to the little one?"

"No, Morrigan. She is under my protection. We both know that you chose not to take sides. You are neither of the light nor the dark. You enjoy both life and death. Orabella will not be a part of any schemes you bring to her."

"But she is powerful, and I would love to be aligned with such power." Morrigan stared at me as she spoke.

"You must leave now, Morrigan," Opa said with a strength I had never heard from him before.

Morrigan floated closer to me, while Opa stood between us.

"Whatever your Opa tells you about Iblis, it is nothing compared to the darkness that awaits you. Just remember: if you ever need help, I am here—perhaps even to get your parents back."

"Wait. How do you know about my parents?"

"I've been watching you. You need to stay away from that boy, Theom."

The fear I had experienced at the summer solstice came surging back to me. I tried to ask Morrigan more, but before I could even open my mouth, the wind picked up in the room. The desk and the pedestal and the chairs shook as the wind gusted past them. My hair flew around my face, making it hard to see what was happening. The lights dimmed and brightened as the whistling of the wind became almost deafening. I held onto my grandfather as I was nearly lifted off my feet. I kept my eyes glued to Morrigan, even with my hair gathering in front of my face.

Three lines of light grew from her chest and expanded to the length of her body, and as they grew brighter, I almost had to shield myself from watching. Then, the lights went out, and she was gone. The room settled. All that was left was an earthy smell that hung dank in the air.

"We need to get her back if she can help my parents return."

"That's a bad idea. Yes, Morrigan may help, but it comes at a great cost. One of us would have to die as payment."

"How did she hear us, Opa? Are you or Oma going to die?"

"Orabella, that isn't going to happen. Morrigan is powerful and can be a great ally, but never trust her. I have never asked for any favours from her, and I advise you to do the same. If she offers you advice or insight, only accept it if she is willing to part with it for free. She can be helpful, but she is not a friend."

I once again felt afraid. *How could someone offer advice and expect something as great as death in return? That seems evil! How could any being be worse than that?*

"Will you tell me more about Iblis?"

Opa turned to me and replied, "Let's sit down again and get comfortable."

We moved back to our chairs. I tried to put Lolo in my lap, but she was consumed with sniffing around the spot Morrigan had disappeared from.

Opa began, "The spirit Iblis is a Jinn, the name for the original genies, who are mischievous spirits of the Earth.

They reside in a universe parallel to the human world while maintaining the ability to interact in both realms."

"Like a genie in a bottle?" I asked him.

"Yes, the same type, but these genies do not grant you three wishes. Instead, they feed off those wishes you make."

"So, they live in a different apartment level but have an elevator on our level?"

"Yes, something like that. I'm happy you understand the concept. The Jinn came into creation over twenty-five thousand years ago. They lived in a different dimension from ours but found our planet early in its existence and fed off the fears and superstitions of the early people.

"It was Horus who stood up to the Jinn and battled them for our protection, but Horus made an agreement with Iblis during their battle to prevent them from losing. That agreement stated that the Jinn could travel between their dimension and ours, but the Jinn could not directly interfere with humans. Because we have free will, we're still capable of making our own choices.

"However, the Jinn can persuade those choices, and they can control us if we give them permission. Unlike other beings in the universe, they can draw power from the other celestials like fairies, angels, and demons. They can thrive throughout the different dimensions, and Iblis has spent many centuries stealing the inspiration that feeds the Tree of Life."

As Opa told me this story, I felt like I already knew it, like I had already confronted Iblis—or I soon would. I felt my stomach tighten.

"If the Soljourner is the light, and Iblis is dark, then what is the darkness?"

"Darkness is all around us. It's the empty space between the light. We, as Soljourners, must keep the balance between the dark and the light. That is the one true principle of life: balance. It is written in the Book that the last Soljourner shall fight the final battle against Iblis and the darkness."

I stared at Opa, my eyes wide. I could not imagine myself being the one to fight such an evil being. I grabbed Lolo from her place at my feet and squeezed her tightly. She meowed a little bit to show me she understood.

Then, a low knock came at the wooden door, and Oma pushed it open, carrying two cups of tea into the Shoe Chamber. She put them down on the desk and leaned over Opa to kiss him. "How are you both doing?" Oma's voice was bright and cheery.

"This is so freaking awesome, Oma. There's a lot to learn, but it's so fascinating," I said enthusiastically, pushing away the thoughts of a final battle with Iblis.

Opa was quiet and smiled at Oma.

"Yes, everything's going quite well," he said.

"I brought you some chamomile tea. It's getting late, so I'm going to bed," Oma said.

"I don't feel tired at all! Oma, are you a Soljourner that can time travel too?" I asked her eagerly.

"No, Bella, I am your Opa's sidekick. But I am heading off to bed to read. How long will you be staying up?" Oma asked.

I looked at Opa, hopeful he would not retire for the night.

"We'll continue until this girl over here passes out in her seat," Opa said, still smiling.

"I guess I'll see you both at breakfast, then," Oma said. She grabbed a blanket from the couch and draped it over me and kissed me on my cheek. She then walked over to Opa's chair and kissed him before heading out the door and back up the stairs.

The air was heavy in the underground Shoe Chamber, but it was comfortable under the blanket, and the tea was helping to warm up my belly. I leaned back in my chair and looked at the ceiling. I began to study the shadows and realized the roof of the Shoe Chamber was covered in roots—almost like we were under a tree!

No, it couldn't be! Like in the dream?

"Opa, are these the roots from the tree outside my bedroom window?"

Opa leaned forward and said, "Yes, the tree above us was first planted by your great-grandfather. He did it to protect us. It shields us from Iblis and any other dark forces. Each Soljourner has been protected by this type of tree."

"We don't have a tree like this at my house."

"Your dad didn't want one at the house. He tried to keep all the things I have here far away from you, trying to protect you from the history of our family. He wanted to be the last Soljourner so he could protect you from what our paths as Soljourners foretell. We have to follow the guidelines and instructions given to us. He wanted to do things on his terms—on his own time. Unfortunately, that's not how our job works. We have a great amount of responsibility that requires us to do the bidding of others for the greater good. It's a lot to undertake, but it is worthwhile, for the Tree of Life is the most powerful essence of all that exists."

As Opa finished his sentence, a warm wind swirled into the room. *Was Morrigan back?* Instead, someone else appeared beside Opa. It was my friend, Ara . . . except it wasn't quite Ara. *Oh boy, we have another visitor.* Her whole body—not just her eyes—was glowing green, but what was just as unnerving as her glowing was that none of the green reflected into the room. It was like she was encased in green. A strong smell of daisies filled the room.

"Hello, Wadjet. Pleasure meeting you here in this dimension," Opa said.

"Yes, human, there have been many dream-state conversations, but I must be here, as Orabella needs to work with me and the amulet. There is too much at stake," Wadjet said in an echoing voice that didn't bounce off the walls but seemed to be echoing within her own body.

"Why now? You've never interfered before. You've always allowed the Soljourners to train from each other. Is it because she is the last of our kind?" Opa asked.

"Yes, this little one is the last of your kind, but what also makes Orabella special is that she is female, and soon she will be born into womanhood," Wadjet said, as if speaking at the bottom of a great canyon, the reverberations bouncing in my ears.

I reached over to grab Opa's hand. What did she mean that I would be born into womanhood?

"Wadjet, we were all aware of that when Orabella was born. You and I have worked together in Dreamtime to prepare her for her destiny. I thought there would be no interference from the goddesses."

"Things have changed. There is a new foe," Wadjet replied. "Other than Iblis and the darkness?" I asked nervously.

Opa gripped my hand tightly. "What do you mean? Is it Morrigan? Because we just had a visit from her."

"No," Wadjet replied, "an enemy from within. I do not want to say who it is at this point. I must take this child with me now and spend time with her."

"Why can't you work in Dreamtime with her since she is protected there?" Opa asked suspiciously.

"No! We both know that Dreamtime is the space between all things, and her spirit body is vulnerable there. Her spirit body is strong. Now we need to strengthen her mind."

"Wait a minute, don't I get to choose?" I inserted myself into their conversation.

"I'm afraid not," Wadjet said with echoing finality.

9

TIMELESS TREE—JULY 2ND–3RD, (SOMEWHERE IN TIME)

"Wait!" I blurted out, but Opa, Wadjet, and the Shoe Chamber were gone. I could only sense a swirling motion, like seasickness, as I travelled down a green tube of light that swirled all around me. There was no sound, just the green light. The swirling stopped, and I bent over, feeling like I was about to throw up. I opened my eyes and saw outer space. I took a cautious look above me. There were stars, planets, and suns all around, but when I looked below me, I was standing on water. Somehow, it seemed stable. I reached down to touch it, and warm water ran through my fingers. I pulled my hand from the water and looked directly in front of me. It was the glowing tree from my dreams. Reflected in the water below was an upside-down tree that was joined at the trunk.

"Orabella, you stand before the Tree of Life, and you are the only human to have ever done so."

I was so in awe of everything around me that I had forgotten about Wadjet. I turned to face her.

"But where is this?"

"You are standing at the centre of all creation. This is what you humans call the 'Big Bang' explosion, where life began. From it, two trees were born that brought life to all beings. The Tree of Life and Tree of Knowledge are joined but separate. The Tree of Life connects different life forms. The Tree of Knowledge connects heaven and the underworld. Both Trees are associated with the Creator: the trunks are the bodies, the branches are the minds with their beliefs and dreams, and the roots are the connections to each other and the Earth.

"The Tree of Life is the female entity, which brings us inspiration, creativity, art, and imagination. The Tree of Knowledge is the male entity, which brings us logic, analytical thought, science, and math."

"Oh boy, I do *not* think the Tree of Knowledge is my friend. I suck at math and science," I said with a giggle, which Wadjet did not acknowledge. I glanced around awkwardly.

Wadjet spoke again. "Since before you were born, Iblis has gone back in history and focused on harming women on your planet because feminine energy helps feed the Tree of Life. That's why, from the time of Egypt to this present moment, women have always been viewed as lesser.

"Iblis has used his powers to rid society of the balance of god and goddess. The time has come to right the imbalance—not only with the uprising in the fight for equality, but also through your role as the first female Soljourner."

"Why me? I have hypermobility, which makes me clumsy. I also have ADHD, dyslexia, and social anxiety, and I'm awkward most of the time. I don't know if any of that makes me more prepared to be the protector of the Tree of Life."

"Those are labels of human conditions, but you should consider them gifts. It has made you more than who you are. These differences have made you stronger, for you have persevered and adapted to your situations. And being the first female, you have been granted other gifts as well. You can see what is happening in all aspects of time, and you can feel the changes that Iblis creates. The cycle of the Soljourner may have come to an end, but you are female. You can create a new cycle, a new type of Soljourner to protect the Tree of Life," said Wadjet.

"I don't understand. What, then, is the point of all this if it feels like one step forward, two steps back? From what I have been told by my Opa, we have done and sacrificed so much. Why is there so much evil and pain in the world today? And it feels like it keeps getting worse," I replied, confused all over again as I paced back and forth on the water. I started scratching at my arm, as I felt emotionally overwhelmed, trying not to think about going to the bathroom.

Wadjet stood beside the Tree of Life, floating just above the water. "Like the waves on the seashore, there's an ebb and flow of the tides, which are controlled by something that is outside of the Earth. Very much like the waves, we are just a part of the process and don't know the grand scheme. Things happen, and we may not know why, but it slowly prepares us for something bigger. Each Soljourner has had the very same mission, and each task has turned out differently. There is no winning or losing, but there is always growth. We must abide by the laws of time and balance. Light and dark cannot live without the other."

I was angry and suddenly shouted, "That is B.S.!"

Wadjet looked surprised, and her form quivered for a moment. Her form seemed disturbed by my intense energy, like she was having a hard time staying in Ara's body. I was embarrassed that I lashed out but continued nevertheless, "Then what is the point of free will or having the imagination to design our future through our potential?"

Wadjet was still, but my focus wasn't on her anymore. My eyes wandered to the beauty that surrounded us. There was an energy around this place that was warm and loving. The Tree and the shining stars of the galaxy were shrouded in beautiful colours.

Wadjet spoke. "That is exactly why we have come to this moment. You are at a pivotal point where you can reassert the feminine energy that has not been a part of this process. The Soljourners before you have only been given the mission to protect your history, but you are capable of bigger things. You are also one of the youngest chosen, which allows you to stay in touch with your imagination, possibilities, and inspiration. You still believe in the impossible."

She looked at the Tree and continued, "It is through our imagination that inspiration arises with a feeling that anything is possible. Without it, we have no hope."

"I'm confused. You say I am moving into womanhood, but I'm powerful because I'm a child?"

"You are both. You are growing up, but you still retain your childlike energy of believing in the impossible."

"But why me? Of all the girls in my world and all the other worlds, why me?"

"You have been chosen, and it has taken millennia to get to this point. That is why it is essential to know your heritage. You must understand where you come from. That knowing starts with discovering your roots. Understanding your family tree and the story that goes with it helps you find your own story in the world, your destiny.

"All Soljourners before you have had partners who have helped them. They were women who are most often educators—highly intelligent, but also highly creative. Like your Oma. They work as a team."

"Wait a minute, are you telling me that my mom is my dad's partner in helping him with his missions?"

Wadjet was quiet for a moment before she spoke. "Your human father chose to take a different path, the power of free will, which is neither right nor wrong."

"Are my mom and dad on a mission now? Is that why they disappeared?"

"I do not know. I have received very little information regarding your parents' whereabouts, but I am focusing on you, as I feel a cycle is ending and a new beginning is upon us."

"So, there is the Tree of Life, but what about the Tree of Knowledge?"

Wadjet smiled and pointed to the reflection in the water below the Tree of Life. "The Tree of Life is balanced by the Tree of Knowledge, so one affects the other."

I was about to say something when the water beneath my feet began to shake. It sounded like the Tree was crying as waves of light filtered beneath the bark. Scared, I asked Wadjet, "What's going on?"

"There is a time disturbance, which is affecting the Tree of Life. I need to send you back so I can investigate. But I will return soon to continue your studies."

Before I could speak, I was back in the Shoe Chamber with Opa. "Wadjet, you can't take her!" he yelled desperately.

"She already did, Opa," I replied and started to giggle.

"She did? Where did you go?"

"This cool place at the centre of the universe."

"You went where?"

"It's where the Tree of Life is, a place I've visited many times in my dreams—the ones I told you about, with the golden falcon—but it is way cooler in real life."

"Oh," Opa said, looking embarrassed. "Where is Wadjet now?"

"She brought me back because she says there was a time disturbance, but she will come back to get me soon."

I felt a strong desire to go look in the shoe compartments that lined the room.

10

SHOE TRAVEL – JULY 2ND, 10:00 PM

Scarlett's voice popped into my head with one of her old puns: "I went out for a run this morning and tripped. I may have been wearing the wrong size shoes, but I haven't seen the footage yet." I giggled to myself.

"So, what is the point of these shoes and these cards? Why do you have so many of them? How does this tie into the rest of the story?" I asked Opa. I wanted to know everything now; I wanted to put the last piece of the puzzle in its place.

Opa walked towards the wall with a wide grin on his face. He reached into one of the shoe compartments and picked out a shoe. It was a beautiful ballet slipper. It was a light rose colour, but it did not look like a modern ballet shoe.

He turned to me and said, "We think of shoes as everyday vehicles for life, and there is an infinite variety of them. They have the potential to open doors. They also help us transform and take on a different persona. Some help us tap into our inner power. Shoes have played major roles in stories, including the story of Rhodopis, which has lasted many centuries and has been retold in newer versions. The Soljourner's path was started by a pair of shoes created by Horus. Can you think of another famous pair of shoes?"

"Of course. It was the ruby slippers that Dorothy wore," I said proudly.

"Dorothy's ruby slippers were initially silver, representing our connection to the spirit while remaining grounded."

"Wow, I didn't know that. Is the writer of the *Wizard of Oz* a Soljourner like us?" I asked.

Opa grinned and said, "I am happy you are listening. Yes, he was. From the beginning, Horus granted the Soljourners the ability to become shoe crafters, designers, writers, and cobblers. There were times we became famous in our endeavours, which was not always the wisest move, as it brought us out of the shadows and made it easy for Iblis to find. We have mostly stayed hidden, often protected by the seeds of the Tree of Life. But coming back to the shoes here, all of these shoes are different and special. These shoes came from the people and places that we have helped in our journeys."

"So, will I get to know all about these shoes and where they came from?" I asked.

Opa held up the ballet slipper. "Yes. The shoes within this room will guide you to that exact place in time. It will also bring you back to this correct location, so you mustn't lose the shoe during your travel. There's no time limit on the other side, so take whatever time is needed to complete your mission. You could use it; however, the more time you spend in a place, the more you will forget about your own time and where you came from."

"That's scary! What if I like it so much that I don't want to leave?"

"Well, that's a possibility, but you must always remember why you went there. We often get attached to what makes us feel comfortable or excited, which distracts us from our long-term goal, but with much preparation and practice, your missions will be successful. Discipline is required for your learning, which your dad wasn't very good at" Opa trailed off.

I looked up and asked, "What if I go to a place where I don't understand the language? Or what if they dress differently there and I stand out?"

"Well, this is where the stone comes in. The magic and knowledge are passed on from the Book to the stone. The stone will give you the information you need to blend into your surroundings."

"Like a cloaking device?" I suggested. "So why do I still need to be schooled and learn languages and skills like from goddesses and Oma?" I was hoping to myself I wouldn't have to go back to school again.

"No matter how many tools you have to assist you, it's important to educate yourself, which is partly why you would be homeschooled by Oma, but also by the goddesses. You will learn that Knowledge is power. You can't know everything, but the more you learn, and with the assistance and trust of your intuition, you will be greatly prepared for any mission that will come your way—as a Soljourner and as a human."

"So, the girls that were in the kitchen this morning when I ran off—they are goddesses?"

"Yes, those girls are just two of many cultural goddesses of the world. Since their power is dependent upon the belief we have in them, their level of power can be limited. Not only will they help teach you about the culture that they are from, but they can also grant you temporary powers to help you defeat Iblis. They show up looking like people we know so it doesn't startle us and so we won't be overwhelmed by their original forms, which can come in a variety of shapes, both beautiful and frightening."

"Wow. I'm going to have magical powers?"

I jumped up and threw a fist pump. Opa didn't seem amused, so I sat back down in my chair sheepishly. He looked at me and continued:

"Goddesses are mythical warriors from one of the twelve dimensions I've spoken of. Georgia is the Chinese goddess, Didu Mu, who supervises the registry where all births and deaths are recorded. She's also known as the goddess of light. As for Scarlett, she is Chalchiuhtlicue, the Aztec goddess of running water and springs, rivers, and lakes. She brings fertility to crops. Her name means 'woman of the jade skirt.' Remember, other people can see the goddesses too, so be careful what you say to them around other people."

I laughed. "What is it with green? We have a green Egyptian goddess, a green book, a green stone, and now a green Aztec goddess. Is there a green cat?" I said sarcastically as I looked down at Lolo, who was napping by my feet.

"Hmm. Well, the colour green relates to balance and harmony. Ultimately, that is your journey. You have Georgia, who will light your way, and Scarlett, who will help with balance. Everything is tied together for a reason. Iblis and the forces of chaos are very powerful, and the disharmony they have created over time has only made them stronger. These girls are two of the fifty-two who would help you on your journeys."

"Why fifty-two? That's so oddly specific."

"The Eye of Horus granted each Soljourner the ability to go on fifty-two missions. Then, the knowledge and experience of each mission were to be transferred to the Emerald Book.

"So, what do the shoes, mythical goddesses, and missions have in common?"

"Each goddess is related culturally to the historical woman that you will be helping. The same thing with each shoe. Up until now, the male Soljourners have been helped by male gods and have helped male historical figures." Opa went over to another shoe compartment and pulled out a combat boot. "For example, I used these to travel back in time to help General Charles de Gaulle. Iblis had him kidnapped, and without his leadership, the Nazis could have overtaken France and defeated them in this timeline, which would have changed the course of history."

"Who is General Charles de Gaulle?"

"He led the French resistance against Nazi Germany and restored order in France after World War II. He was the architect of their new constitution and became president in 1958. If his accomplishments had been removed, our history could have changed for the worse."

"Which god helped you and gave you powers?"

"The god Sucellus helped me by allowing me to use his magic cauldron to locate the general, who was hidden behind a cloud of darkness. Wars throughout history have been pivotal points for Iblis in his quest to destroy the Tree of Knowledge. Since before you were born, Iblis has been trying to kill the Tree.

"If Horus had continued his battle with Iblis, the human realm would have been destroyed. By banishing Iblis to his rightful dimension, Horus did not annihilate the problem. Instead, he saved millions of human lives. He made his own personal sacrifice for the greater good," Opa said.

Opa stood up out of his chair and stretched his back. Lolo then hopped off of my lap and did her cat stretch.

"I think this is a good time for a break. Let's eat some food and catch some sleep. Tomorrow will be a new day full of lessons. Orabella, your destiny is the beginning and end of this story. Your ancestors that have come before you have laid the groundwork. They've gained the knowledge from their own mistakes and journeys. You have all the tools in front of you to help you finish our family's role as Soljourners. You have the protection of the Tree, the wisdom of the Emerald Book, and the power of the amulet. You also have the lessons from each of these shoes provided to you by the Journey Cards that go with each shoe, and lastly, you will have the capabilities that the goddess girls will lend to you on each mission."

11

LEARNING DAY–JULY 2ND

"Your first journey will be an initiation to where the Soljourners were born, because you can't see your future until you have understood your past."

"Wadjet said that same thing to me. She said that I needed to know where I came from." I started thinking about Horus and suddenly felt the weight and responsibility of what I'd chosen to do. *How would I ever be ready? Am I the one? What happens if I fail?*

I peeled myself off of my chair and walked out of the Shoe Chamber. Lolo twisted around my ankles as we climbed the spiral staircase back to the workshop. As we ascended the stairs, I noticed that my feelings were slowly becoming less intense, like I was being unplugged from something. We passed through the work area and opened the door to the night sky. Oma suddenly appeared with some tea.

"I thought I would bring you both some chamomile tea before I headed off to bed," Oma said.

Had we been downstairs that long? I looked at Opa, who said, "Yes, Audrey, sounds good. We can have it in the kitchen before getting ready for bed."

"Did you cover a lot then?" Oma asked.

"Yes, and Orabella absorbed a lot of information."

"Oh good, and how are you feeling, Orabella?"

"I'm happy to know the truth now and excited to learn more."

"Okay, well, I'm going to bring the tea in the house and get ready for bed. Good night you two." Oma walked back to the house. Opa and I stayed a little behind her.

"What just happened? Oma brought tea to us a little while ago," I said to Opa.

"Sometimes, there are subtle time fluctuations when you're around the Emerald Tablet. Time almost always slows down, but it can also go backwards."

"Weird! Have you told Oma this?"

"Yes, I have. Your Oma is very aware of time fluctuations; however, when they do happen, I never mention it since it can be very confusing," Opa replied with a kind smile directed at Oma.

"I totally get that."

So many thoughts and questions turned in my head. Every emotion and belief intertwined, like riding a roller coaster. Opa reached out, held my hand tightly, and led us towards the big tree on our way back into the house. When we arrived at the tree, he pressed my hand against the bark.

"This tree protects us from being found and holds off any energy that may be seeking the Book. It's still quite a young tree, like yourself. It has seen beautiful sunny days and horrible storms, but through it all, it has stayed rooted and strong. It flows with the wind but remains strong enough to stand up against it."

As Opa spoke, I continued to ride the roller coaster of emotions. I felt excited, like a superhero ready to protect and save the world, but it was much bigger than that. I was a protector of the Tree of Life.

Then, Opa looked at me and asked, "What do you think the *Wizard of Oz* was about?"

I looked at Opa quizzically with the sudden change of topic, but I answered, "Well, from what I remember, and from what my dad tells me, it's what they call a 'hero's journey.' Dorothy goes on a journey to find herself and . . . wait a minute, are Dorothy's slippers in the Shoe Chamber?" I said with quiet excitement.

"A version of them are, but not the ones from the story."

"It feels like my own fairy tale!"

"Yes, a more dangerous one with many more consequences attached to it. Dorothy's story was created to inspire girls at that time to feel empowered. To rise and become leaders in their communities, cities, and countries. Many of the shadow forces tried to downplay the author and hide the messages that he was trying to convey secretly in fairy tales. These stories about the hero's journey are another tool to inspire us. But the fact remains that you are the last Soljourner, and this is just the beginning of the ending where a new path, a new story will be created."

Again, that was what Wadjet already said to me. It was like they were connected.

I nodded my head. There were no more words to say. I would only understand things as they happened.

Opa smiled and kissed me on the forehead. "Let's rest up. It has been a long day. You did very well today."

"I am going to go have a bath instead, Opa. I am way too energized to go to bed," I said as I gave him a big hug.

"Okay, Bella, sleep well," Opa said, and he turned to go up the stairs to his bedroom.

12

BAD DREAM—JULY 2ND, 10:30 PM

While I was having a bath, I drank Oma's second cup of tea she had brought us. I thought about everything that had happened today, including going to the centre of the universe. *How cool was that?* After a while, I got out, dried myself off, put on my pyjamas, and then headed to bed. I felt proud of myself. It was very grown-up of me to be taking on so much responsibility. My mind was going a million kilometres an hour, and my body buzzed, but when I climbed into bed, the tiredness washed over me. My body sank deep into sleep. A heaviness overtook me as I lay there, and I felt myself falling.

The golden falcon was flying in a circle above the Tree of Life, but it kept soaring higher and higher, as if it would fly away from the Tree and into the sun. As the falcon flew out of sight, the brightly colored yellow and red leaves of the Baobab began to fall off of its branches. The Tree started to wither. The Tree of Life was dying. I panicked but couldn't move. I watched my dream fall apart. I felt powerless and cold. I screamed soundlessly. My body seemed to be turning to dust as quickly as the Tree. The falcon soon disappeared, and complete darkness overtook me. Then, in front of me, I saw red eyes peering from all around me in the darkness. I tried to push away from the eyes and run, but I still couldn't move.

And then, the eyes winked out, and what took their place was a fire that burned all around me. The Tree was burning, and I was crying, asking myself, *What can I do?* Then, laughter filled my head, overtaking all other thoughts, and dark, slimy hands with long fingers reached out of the water, climbing up my body. They stretched higher and higher towards my face to pull me under. I felt the hands grasp me, and the water came up around me. I held my breath to protect myself from drowning.

Wait. I calmed my mind despite the clawing hands and ash burning all around me, choking me. I let go of the laughter in my head and focused on my breath. I allowed myself to sink into the water. I breathed deeply, taking it in, feeling it all: the fear, the lack of control, the sense of helplessness. Then, suddenly, complete calm and silence came over me. I was floating in the water rather than drowning in it. I breathed normally. I sank deep beneath the water, allowing the nothingness to exist.

I woke up, and the sun was shining brightly in my room. I slowly dragged myself out of bed and went to the kitchen. I felt out of sorts; the sun was already across the sky as if it were afternoon. I walked out on the balcony and saw Oma coming in from the shed. She smiled and said, "Finally awake, sleepyhead? Opa felt it was best that you slept. We figured you would get hungry enough eventually to come downstairs and eat."

"How long did I sleep, Oma?"

Oma laughed. "You've been asleep for two days!"

"What? I've never slept so long in my life! How is that possible?"

"Well, you did stay up late with Opa, and you were around the energy of the Emerald Tablet for a while. It can take a lot out of you at first, so if you want to eat something and go back to bed, then you can do so. Take all the time you need."

"Where is Opa?" I asked, still shocked that I slept so long.

"He's in the workhouse. He's trying to catch up on some work."

I made myself some toast with strawberry jam. It seemed like it took forever to eat. I chewed each bite so slowly that I barely had enough energy to swallow it down. I wanted to go back upstairs, but it seemed so far, so I slouched down on the couch and cuddled up there. *Just for a few minutes.*

I fell back into a deep sleep, past the point of the nightmare. I went to the place where I was floating. That beautiful, gentle place.

But even in that gentle place, I suddenly became cold, and two red eyes opened up wide and stared straight at me.

"I know who you are. There is no escaping me. I have your parents, and I will get you too." I knew this voice to be that of Iblis.

I woke up screaming and saw Oma and Opa looking over me. I looked around. It was nighttime, and I was in my bed. I was baffled.

"Are you okay?" Opa asked.

"I thought I fell asleep on the couch?"

Oma looked confused. "Not today, Bella. Yesterday you did."

"You mean I slept away another day?"

"Yes, we wanted you to rest. Don't be alarmed," Oma said.

I was scared because I didn't know if I was dreaming again or if this was real.

Opa spoke to me, calmly, "Orabella, breathe. Wiggle your toes and feel your body. You're back in the real world. You're safe."

I took long, deep breaths. I moved my toes and felt the bed underneath me and the weight of Lolo on my chest. I began to calm down.

"I think I had a dream about Iblis. There were red eyes. I also dreamt that Horus flew away, and the Tree of Life was burning."

Opa said, "I was afraid of that. I think Iblis found you because your power has grown, and he can sense it. For now, you will sleep in the Shoe Chamber under the Tree. What do you think, Oma?"

"Yes, Jasper, I think you're right. Don't worry, Bella. We're all here for you. Lolo will go with you too."

I got up and got dressed, and we went to the Shoe Chamber, where Opa pulled the hideaway bed out from the couch.

"Many nights I've had to sleep here myself. When you feel rested up, we shall continue. Here, under the tree, you'll be safe in your dreams."

Oma and Opa started their climb up the spiral staircase and began chatting once they were at the top, thinking that

I could not overhear them. I heard Oma say, "I thought Lolo was supposed to protect her in Dreamtime?"

"Yes, I thought so, too," said Opa.

"What happened? Have you had any contact from Horus at all?"

"No. The falcon that flew back with us and circled the tree the other day was the only sign I've seen or heard from him since he visited us last. She will be safe here under the tree. The energy from the amulet will protect her."

"This seems much bigger than we thought, Jasper. I'm afraid of what her future holds."

"Yes, it is a little concerning. There seems to be a lot of things going on that we're not aware of."

"Have you gotten any information as to where Mary and Marcus are?" Oma asked him, hopefully.

"No, not yet, but Morrigan tells me that they're still alive."

"What? She was here too?" Oma asked in surprise.

"Yes, she appeared before Wadjet did. Things are happening too quickly. Have the other two goddesses gotten back to you?"

"Not since they were here the other day. Jasper, I feel there's a sense of urgency. We need to help her but also protect her."

Opa replied, "Yes, Audrey, I agree, but I don't know how."

The conversation was now off in the distance. I felt myself being pulled back into a dream. I drifted on the cosmic water under the Tree of Life. I felt protected and safe. The water rocked me back and forth like I was a baby in a crib. I let go and fell asleep within my dream.

I awoke refreshed and renewed. It was the first time in a long time that I couldn't remember anything about my dreams. I looked up and saw the roots of the trees coming through the ceiling. There was only one light on, which was on the stone desk where Opa was working. He looked over and brought me a glass of water.

He sat down at the foot of the bed and took off his glasses. "I need you to tell me every detail of what happened to you in your dreams."

As I began to tell him, his eyebrows twitched while he hung on to every word.

"Iblis said that he has Mom and Dad."

"Iblis is also a liar and a great deceiver, so you never know. He mixes fact with lies to gain the upper hand. Once your emotions cloud your intuition and judgment, he will lead you down the wrong path. If you have a dream within a dream, a slip within the fabric of realities, it allows him to manipulate you and distract you from the truth."

"Has he ever come to you this way?" I asked, my heart pounding in my chest.

"No, he hasn't, but I know that my grandfather, your great-great-grandfather, could be weak of spirit and would inadvertently allow Iblis in to distract him from his mission. And because of this, Iblis almost killed him. Since then, I've been strict with myself and your father. I've been strict with my teachings and with my self-assuredness. Being sure with one's self is the key to keeping Iblis at bay. You can't let him sway your thoughts. You can't let him cloud your pathway with doubt. For everything created out of goodness and light, there's a lot of evil and darkness—it's the natural law of balance. Within hate is love; within peace is war. But let me not get into it too deeply. What would you like to eat so we can begin your training?"

"Anything, Opa. I'm starving!"

"Okay, I'll be right back with breakfast."

I got up and followed Opa up the stairs.

"Hey, where do you think you're going?"

"I need to go to the bathroom. Is that okay?"

"Yes, of course, but take Lolo with you." He looked back at her. "Can you come and protect Bella while she's in the bathroom?"

Lolo looked up and began to climb the stairs behind us.

"Opa, she listened to you like she knew what you were saying."

"Yes, she did listen. She's here to protect you."

"What is she, Opa? You mentioned that she is a special cat. What kind of cat is she?"

"Let me get your breakfast, and when I return, I will tell you."

Opa left, and I went into the bathroom. I could see Lolo's shadow pacing outside the door. I finished and headed back down the stairs with Lolo right behind me. As I stepped down the spiral staircase, I once again felt a strange, tingling sensation.

Opa returned with blueberry pancakes and bacon, which I inhaled. Between breaths, I asked Opa, "Why do I have this strange feeling like I'm being plugged in every time I come into this room?"

"Anybody who comes into this room is being plugged into the power of the Emerald Tablet. They give off an energy that connects us to their information."

"Like it takes over my body? Why didn't you warn me?" I asked in a tense voice.

"You're okay for now since you haven't touched the Book or worn the necklace. Learning to harness their powers will be part of your training. They contain a huge amount of energy—the energy of the universe that formed life itself. Part of being able to harness their powers will also include disciplining your emotions and mind."

I felt a little freaked out thinking about it, but Opa started talking again.

"As you grow in knowledge and maturity, so will your powers, and so will the complexity of your adventures. Many of the experiences you will be going on initially will be focused on historical heroines around the same age. It could also include obscure heroes from the past that time has forgotten, even if they made a significant impact on society. Let's take, for example, Marie Camargo, the real creator and innovator of modern ballet. Marie was the first woman to execute the intricate entrechat quatre, a jump where the dancer scissors her legs four times in the air. Marie is also said to have invented the 180-degree turnout.

"Another thing that she did to influence dance was to change the heeled shoes in ballet to slippers. She also shortened her ballet skirt. All of these things are still used in ballet today. You may have to go back to Paris in 1726 to help prevent any potential modifications to this narrative."

"Wow, I love ballet, and now I can go meet Marie Camargo?"

"Well, I think it's best if I show you."

13

NO TOWER–JULY 6TH, 9:20 AM

"Let's go on a little field trip."

Opa walked over to the far wall of the Shoe Chamber where all the shoes were stored in their individual compartments. He reached into one of the compartments and pulled out the ballet slipper that he had shown me previously.

I took a moment to examine the room around me. The wooden pedestal with the Emerald Book was in the middle of the room. It was facing the two old leather, high back chairs to the right of the wall filled with shoes. There was a retro 70s couch with an ugly flower pattern on it. That was the couch I slept on. On the far wall was an old desk with lots of books from the bookshelf above. To the left of the desk was the door that opened to the spiral staircase. There was an earthy smell from the exposed roots above us, and I wondered if this was how Hobbits felt living in an underground home. Opa took out the necklace from his pocket and put it on, and a flash of green lit up the stone like a firefly.

"Opa, what are you doing?" I asked nervously, my eyes fixed on the pendant of his necklace.

Opa took my hand, and I heard a loud *whoosh* like I was in a windstorm. I felt sick to my stomach and a little dizzy. When the whooshing stopped, I looked around and instantly realized we were not at home anymore. There were old stone buildings everywhere. Then, I heard Opa's voice.

"Welcome to Paris, France, May 5th, 1726. The day that Marie Camargo makes her performance debut in Paris."

"You've got to be kidding me. Really?" I exclaimed in a foreign language. It sounded a lot like French. My eyes got wide at the realization that I wasn't speaking English.

Opa must have known what I was thinking because he replied, "Yes, both you and I are speaking Parisian French, but in our heads, we still hear English."

"That is so cool! It's the stone that allows this?"

"Yes, but it's still important to learn different languages! In case you ever lose the necklace, you'll need a backup plan. It's important to be able to communicate with those around you."

I was trying to pay attention to what he was saying, but I was blown away by my sudden ability to speak French and by the incredible scenery all around me. I had never been to Paris, even in my own time.

Sensing that I wasn't listening, Opa decided we should press on with our journey. "Okay, well, we better get to the theatre and watch the performance. We can't stay too long as the Emerald Necklace can't keep us both here. It's only supposed to be used by one person. Once either of us starts to fade, we will need to leave immediately."

Opa put the ballet slipper in the pocket of his gorgeous, long brown coat. He was dressed like a French royal with a broad hat, pants that only went to his knees, long white stockings, and shoes with big buckles. He looked so regal, so unlike the blue jean overalls he usually wore.

We started heading in a direction that I assumed Opa knew the way of. My head was on a swivel as I attempted to look at everything. "But what about my clothing and money? When did you change into those clothes?"

Opa stopped walking to answer my questions. "There's a safe under my desk by the pedestal in the Shoe Chamber that has money that's been collected by all the Soljourners. Each Soljourner puts money aside to give to the next. There are all types of currency to choose from in there that you can grab in preparation for each mission. To answer your second question, when you look down at yourself, it looks to you like you're wearing your normal clothing, but with the aid of the slipper and the stone, everybody else sees us wearing clothes like them. Wait till we find a mirror. Then you'll see what you're wearing," Opa said.

We started our walk towards the theatre again.

"Opa, how do you know which way to go?"

"Lots of studying and travelling."

I was still trying to take in all the sights. I was so excited to be in Paris.

As we walked, Opa listed off the things I needed to remember. "Before each mission, you'll learn about the culture, the language, and the person you are going to meet. You'll take the appropriate shoe, just like the ballet slipper we took for this journey, and you'll study the Journey Card that has been left for you from the other Soljourners that have travelled to that time period before you. Each trip will have its allies that can help you along the way—like the goddesses with their gifts. You will also have the necklace with you, so if you have any questions, you can use the Emerald Stone to connect to the Book back at home."

As we walked along the cobblestone streets, he continued. "Most importantly, remember to trust yourself and your instincts. Just imagine, without Marie's passion and innovation in ballet, she never would have left her legacy. Would ballet have the same sort of magic it has today without her influence? Inspiration like Marie's is what feeds the Tree of Life. It gives it strength, and from the Tree's strength comes the power that provides humanity's hope. That hope gives rise to faith when darkness is upon us."

I was buzzing with all the information being told to me and with the excitement of the city. We drew close to the theatre, and I noticed there was a gathering of people outside. I chuckled and thought this wasn't so different from going to a concert in my time. Not much had changed.

Opa went up to the ticket booth and requested two tickets. The lady in the booth gave them to him, and he turned around to put mine in my hand. "Now remember: with any items like this, only money can be returned to our time to be used later. Do you understand? This is very important, as it can create what we call a 'future's past moment.'"

"What is that?"

"It's when you take a solid object from one time and bring it to another time. It creates a mini-earthquake in the timeline, which is like two identical cars travelling side by side on a highway, but at any moment, they could crash into each other and destroy both realities."

As we walked through the lobby, I noticed a mirror, which I made a beeline for, eager to see my outfit. I was stunned by my reflection. I wore a sprawling, puffy gown as you would see in a baroque painting. It was yellow with white lace, and on top of my head, I wore a white wig covered by a large, yellow hat that matched my dress. I almost didn't recognize myself.

"Orabella, stop admiring yourself. We need to get to our seats," Opa said with a smile and wink.

I rushed up behind him and asked, "Is that what everybody else sees?" I looked down at myself, and I was wearing my regular clothes: runners, blue jeans, and a blue T-shirt. I didn't look royal at all.

"What you see in the mirror is what everybody else sees, like a mirage."

I looked around at all the people who were dressed so extravagantly. It was as if we were going to a ball. We found our seats at the top balcony on the right side of the stage. I was blown away by the beauty and design of the theatre. The stage was illuminated by six grand chandeliers and by rows of candles in front of the stage. The scenery was lit from the sides by candles. The huge paintings on the walls of the theatre made me feel like I was in a museum. Nothing like this came close to anything I'd seen in Vancouver. As we found our places, a man and a boy sitting in our box with us introduced themselves.

"Good day, my lady. I am Louis de Bourbon, Count of Clermont, and this is King Louis XV."

Oh, my goodness! A king! Do I bow? Do I hold out my hand? I decided to stand and bow, something told me that that was the right thing to do.

The young king asked for my name, but I started to stutter in disbelief that a king should be speaking to me. "I-I-I'm . . ."

Opa leaned in from behind me and replied, "Good day, I'm Jasper of the house of Van Dern Berg, and this is my granddaughter, Orabella."

Opa was so calm, yet I continued to freak out internally. I was meeting a king, even though he was still a boy. Nonetheless, the king kept staring at me, which made my cheeks turn red. I turned to Opa and whispered to him, "I think this boy likes me."

Opa laughed and replied, "Well, Orabella, funny enough, this is in a period in time when you would be the perfect age for marriage."

"Okay, I've heard enough. Let's get this show over with and go home. I don't want to be married off, even if I would become a French queen," I whispered to Opa. I thought of my friends at school, Camille and Lilou, whose parents were from France. I wished I could tell them about this.

King Louis continued to smile at me, which was so awkward, as I had never had a boy interested in me before.

A woman came out on stage and started to sing opera. *Phew, perfect timing.* The boy finally took his eyes off of me and focused on the stage. Soon behind the opera singer, dancers came out to join her on stage. I got shivers from the raw power of the live performance. I didn't want to blink and miss any part of it. *Which one was Marie Camargo?* I thought as I scanned the performers. Then a woman appeared from the wings. Her movements were so graceful and fluid, I instantly knew who it was. Marie stood out amongst the other dancers with her presence, her grace, her power, and her technical ability. I momentarily got distracted when the boy king touched his shoe to mine. I turned to him and glared, and he quickly moved his foot away from mine.

As soon as the ballet was over, Opa said, "Well, now we need to go back to the exact spot that we arrived at."

"Why is that?"

"Because that is what we call a time vortex or portal. It's important to have the shoes you're wearing with us, and the ballet shoe that brought us here. Without it, we can't go back."

"Oh, okay, so exact spot, portal, shoes we came with, and the shoe we carried," I said out loud, trying to remember everything.

"Yes, it's imperative to follow those specific instructions."

I sometimes thought Opa was way too uptight about this. *What's the worst that could happen? Getting stuck in this time? That doesn't seem so bad.* But then, I thought about that boy and getting married. Maybe Opa was right to get out of here.

Opa turned to Louis de Bourbon, Count of Clermont, and King Louis XV to say goodbye.

"Oh, nonsense. You're invited to our gathering to meet the beautiful Marie Camargo. She will be attending as well," Louis de Bourbon said as the young king smiled at me leeringly.

"Thank you for the invitation, but we must hurry to get back to Holland for a special function," Opa said, which did not please the king or Louis de Bourbon. It was probably rare for them to be turned down. The boy king's expression went from surprised to angry.

"I'm sorry, but we must hastily depart," Opa said and grabbed my hand. We quickly descended the stairs from our balcony seats and wove through the crowd. I looked back and saw the king at the top of the stairs with an angry scowl, revealing his age for what it was: a kid having a temper tantrum.

We finally broke free of the crowd and headed for the stairs to the entrance of the theatre. I was hurrying to keep up with Opa's long strides when, from behind us, we heard a loud whistle. We spun our heads around to see the boy king had gathered two police officers to help him stop us from leaving. They were pointing their fingers in our direction and yelling, "Arrêtez! Arrêtez-vous!"

"Oh, boy, I think we may have angered the king," Opa said to me as he grabbed my hand and started moving down the stairs with even more speed. "Let's go, Orabella!"

"Because I didn't like him?" I asked through heavy breathing, trying to keep up.

"Most likely because we turned down their offer. We better get out of here."

We finally reached the bottom of the stairs and arrived in the lobby of the beautiful theatre. Opa started to run, and I was just behind him. We pushed out of the gigantic theatre doors and out into the cobblestone streets. We raced past all the theatre-goers and the beautiful apartments that, just a few hours ago, I was leisurely walking by and admiring. Now I could only focus on getting to our time vortex.

Running on the loose stones proved to be treacherous, and the toe of my sneaker caught in a crack, and I tripped and skidded on my knees and palms. I was stunned after hitting the ground so hard. My palms burned, and my knees were bruised. I looked behind me, and one of my shoes had fallen off in the melee. And even worse, just past my shoe were the police officers racing towards me. This was not good. I needed my shoe to get back home. I was caught between Opa running away from me, and the police and the boy king running towards me. *What do I do?* I started to panic. My heart was pounding and I began to sweat.

The police officers were coming closer, and the boy king was right behind them. They were closing the distance between us, and I could see the king's mouth turn up into a sneering smile. *What to do, what to do?*

I jumped up and ran towards Opa as fast as I could wearing only one shoe. When I reached him, I grabbed the necklace from his neck and turned around to face the police officers and the king. I held the stone in my hands and pointed it directly at them. I took a deep breath and closed my eyes. I followed my breath through my nose, into my lungs, and out through my fingertips into the stone. I focused my energy on the breath I held in my body and then turned my attention outwards. I felt everything slow down all around me. The world quieted, and I opened my eyes. The officers, the king, and even the pedestrians on the sidewalks and in the shops were completely still. I looked back at Opa, and he, too, was frozen. It seemed that even the birds and the insects and the wind had come to a complete standstill. I walked towards my shoe, moving so close to the officers that I could reach out and touch them if I wanted to. I could see the pupils of their eyes wide and determined.

I bent down to pick up my shoe, and when I turned around to return to Opa, my path was blocked by my friend, Camille. Or at least, someone that looked like Camille. She was floating off the ground, which was an obvious clue that she was not Camille but a goddess in her shape. And while everyone else was frozen still, she was able to move.

"Hello, Orabella. It's a pleasure to meet you. Welcome to my country. I am Marianne, goddess of liberty."

"Hi, nice to meet you, Marianne," I said politely, trying to catch my breath from all the excitement.

"Are you in need of my assistance?"

"I'm not sure. This is my first time travel, and I think I made King Louis XV mad."

"Yes, indeed. You turned down the king's advances, which surprised him, and he was embarrassed. I'm impressed with how you have handled yourself."

"Thank you, Marianne," I said, turning my eyes down and curtsying. Oh, my goddess, I love her French accent, and how her words roll off her tongue, and at the same time, how she looks almost exactly like my friend, Camille.

"I have cleared your path to the portal for you. We will soon meet again, as your transformation is coming."

My eyes came back up to meet her, but before I could say anything more, she was gone. Wow, they all vanished like ghosts. I quickly picked up my pace, ran to where Marianne was floating just a moment before, and grabbed Opa by the hand.

"We're going!"

"What?" Opa was moving again and looked very surprised to see me now taking the lead.

"C'mon, Opa!" I had to drag him—he was so taken aback.

"How did you get here? You were just on your hands and knees right there, and now you're here . . ."

"Not now, Opa!" I pulled him out of his trance as I noticed the world around us was also moving again. The officers and the king also had bewildered expressions on their faces.

Opa finally came to his senses when he heard the police officers yelling, "Arrêtez-vous!" again, and he started running towards our exit point with wide eyes. There was just enough distance between the policemen and us before they could follow us into the portal.

We returned to the spot, and again, the windstorm blew all around us. Within moments, we were back in the Shoe Chamber, panting hard from our narrow escape.

"Whew! What just happened, Orabella?" Opa asked excitedly. He continued babbling on, "Did you manage to freeze time? One second you were on the street and the next, you were right next to me! I can't believe you managed to do that! Wow, if you can do that with the necklace, imagine what you'll be able to do with the amulet! Do you want to try it on?"

14

SHINY AMULET—JULY 6TH, 8:00 PM

I stood there, still trying to catch my breath. My eyes widened in disbelief at Opa's mention of trying on the amulet.

"Me? The amulet? Now? I thought I was getting a necklace of yours that was passed on?"

Instead of answering, Opa stood there frozen. He wasn't moving—just like what happened back in Paris. Suddenly, the room felt very different, like the entire Shoe Chamber had been dunked underwater.

I heard a voice behind me say, "Hello, Orabella. I feel it best I teach you how to work the amulet, considering it *is* mine."

I turned around to see who was speaking. It was my friend, Ara, whom I knew to be the form Wadjet took when she was around me. I looked at her then looked back at my Opa nervously.

"Your Opa is safe. I have simply excluded him from this meeting."

I continued looking at my Opa. He had not moved one inch, but he seemed unharmed otherwise. When I looked back at Wadjet, for a split second, I saw her form change. She had shifted from the small brunette friend I knew and loved into what must be her actual form. She was a woman of about eight or nine feet tall, her torso, head, and neck that of a beautiful woman with pale blue skin, but her lower half was that of a giant golden snake. In one hand, she held a golden staff, and at the top of the staff was a round, green emerald surrounded by golden spirals—like the eye of a storm. Her mouth was set tight with no emotion to be read from her face, yet despite this, she was still beautiful.

I only saw her in that shape for a second, for when I blinked, she was back in the form of Ara, and she had one hand hovering over the Book. She then unlatched the stone from the cover of the Book and held it up to me.

I stepped closer to it and saw that the oval amulet was encased by golden clamps that had a swirling design, and I thought that I could hear humming, like how one felt after coming out of a concert. I recognized it as the same sound I had heard in my dreams.

I was captivated by the stone while I stared at it. Then, Wadjet spoke, breaking my enchantment, "By closing your eyes and focusing on the hum of the amulet, you will be able to directly communicate with the Book."

I shook myself to release the hold the amulet had on me and looked Wadjet in her green eyes. "Hold on. Before you say or do anything, I want to know if you've found out anything about my mom and dad."

Ara's form glitched for a moment before she said, "They are alive, from what I can sense. Your parents are in between dimensions in a place called the Void, but it is hard for me to find their exact location."

I tried to gaze at her in Ara's form, but her image kept shifting and shimmering. I would get glimpses of her towering above me with her serpentine body as if she couldn't maintain her guise as the young schoolgirl she pretended to be.

"Why did they disappear? Who took them?"

"It appears your father tried to keep your mother from disappearing from the timeline. Unfortunately, I do not know what would have caused her to disappear," Wadjet replied calmly.

I got angry. "With all your powers, why can't you help them? What about these other goddesses that are supposed to help me with my missions? Can't anyone help me?"

"Orabella, being powerful is one thing, but knowing your limitations is more powerful. Yes, we are powerful, but in our separate dimensions, within our realities. We do not possess those same powers here on your Earth plane. We are limited to what we can do here and in the in-between. Right now, the best way you can help them is by fulfilling your destiny."

Despite her explanation, I still felt like something was missing, a piece of the puzzle that I couldn't put my finger on, but before I could process my speculations, Wadjet came forward and put the amulet on my chest. I felt it clamp onto my sternum, and suddenly a surge of energy ran through me. I felt dizzy and nauseous as the power expanded all around me. A loud ringing developed in my ears. I gulped, feeling the bile rise in my throat. It was then that a burst of light hit my forehead, but it was as if the light was coming from within me at the same time. When I opened my eyes, I was still standing beside Wadjet, but the

Shoe Chamber around me had burst into a million new colours I had never noticed before, and when I closed my eyes, I was transported to a different place. It was like I suddenly walked inside a TV, the information coming from within me and projecting outwards.

"The colours you see are created by the energy that surrounds all living things because the amulet is connected to the Tree of Life."

I wanted to throw up. My stomach was turning. I put a hand over my mouth to try to stop myself from heaving.

"Orabella, remember to wiggle your toes. Feel the ground; imagine breathing into your feet."

I remembered my dream and focused on steadying myself. I breathed and allowed the emotions to go through me instead of buffeting against me like the winds at the top of a mountain.

"This amulet connects you to the Emerald Book, which can give you vast amounts of knowledge, but it can also drive you insane if you are not sure of yourself or your emotions. If you are not careful, it could very easily consume you."

Must keep wiggling my toes, I thought, *or else I fear I will disappear into the stone.* The energy flowing through me made me feel like I had super senses, but the knowledge running through my head was massive and overpowering. It was like I was connected to the internet, and all of its information was being downloaded into me. It was terrifying to receive so much information, but it also came with feelings of confidence, self-assuredness, and power.

Wadjet moved toward me to take the amulet off my chest, but I pulled away. I wanted to feel more. I felt free of all my anxieties, worries, and fears. I felt a freedom I had never felt before.

Wadjet removed the amulet from my chest, and I suddenly felt heavy and sad, because everything turned back to normal. *But what is normal?* My shoulders slumped forward. I felt like crying because now everything seemed so dull and lifeless.

"Please, sit down," Wadjet said.

I felt this pull towards the amulet. I wanted more of that feeling. I wanted to feel the buzz running through my body.

"This amulet is potent. You must not use it until I have taught you how."

"Wadjet, is this what my dad and Opa used for their missions?

"No, all of the Soljourners before you have used the smaller stone that they wore as a necklace. The one you will use has never been worn previously by a human. It was made for you. This amulet chose you."

"How could it choose me?"

"It only came to life after you were born. This amulet was initially a part of the Book."

"But Opa said that the stone comes from the Book. How is this amulet different from the necklace if they're both from the Book?" I looked at the amulet in Wadjet's hands, wanting to be connected to it again.

Wadjet brought over the Book and said, "The stone in the necklace was made from the same material as the tablet, whereas the amulet has always been attached to the Book. It was created with the Book, as was Horus' bidding. It was a completion of a prophecy that when the amulet was released from the Book, it would mark the end of the Soljourner and the beginning of something more powerful."

I felt that I was ready to take on anything at that moment. I felt the power within me growing. I felt myself growing up. I looked over at Opa and saw that he was no longer completely frozen but moving ever so slowly, almost imperceptibly.

My eyes focused back on Wadjet as she spoke. "Orabella, ask Jasper about what happened when you were born. We will meet again soon."

And just like that, she was gone. No one stood before me—neither Ara nor Wadjet—but from across the room, I saw Opa had resumed normal movement. He looked at where I had been standing before Wadjet came then looked at where I was standing presently. He opened his mouth, then closed it, and then opened it again.

"I missed something again, didn't I?"

"Well, Wadjet showed up, you froze, and she introduced me to the amulet."

"Well, it seems she beat me to it then." Opa shrugged, a little exasperated.

"She also said that you have a story to tell me about my birth."

"She had lots to say, it seems."

Opa walked over to a chair and sat down, his arms crossed over his chest in thought. "Well, from what I can remember on the day of your birth, I was working upstairs when I heard a loud humming, but it was a different sound from anything I had ever heard before. Similar to the necklace, but different—deeper, more resonating.

"When I went downstairs to find the source of the sound, the entire room was filled with a bright green glow. I walked over to the Book, where the glowing was brightest, and noticed that the amulet on the cover had unlocked itself. I picked it up and immediately felt it pulse in my hand—stronger than I had ever experienced with the necklace. The pulse was like a heartbeat, and as I felt it thump in my hand, I could also feel it in my chest. I lost myself within its rhythm until I heard your Oma calling for me.

"I quickly put the amulet away in the desk and climbed the stairs to meet her, and that's when she told me you had just been born, so we quickly rushed out of the house to catch the ferry to go meet you."

I smiled; I had never heard this story before.

"The most unusual part of that day was when we left the house to catch the ferry; the roads were empty. The ferry landed, and on the ride to the hospital, it seemed like time stood still. A normal trip from the house to downtown Vancouver with the ferry would take a couple of hours, but on that day, we did it in half the time. We didn't realize it until we got to the hospital, but that was the first time that time had slowed down like that all around us."

I felt my cheeks get hot, and I knew I was blushing. *My birth was so unique.*

"When we got to the hospital room where your mom and dad were, your mom was holding you, and your dad was on the phone. Oma picked you up out of your mother's arms and held you so gently while she stared at you. It was like she was in a trance while she looked at you. Even to this day, Oma feels an unspoken connection with you. When she passed you on to me, I had a feeling that it was somehow different from your dad's birth. When I first held him, I felt scared because I knew the path that lay in front of him, but when I held you, there was a sense of relief. A sense of completion. I was afraid, but I knew you would be taken care of by destiny itself. You were a happy baby, but you are an old soul."

I smiled but felt a sadness as I was reminded of how much I missed my mom and dad.

"So, when we left the hospital and got back to the house, I went back downstairs to the Shoe Chamber to collect the amulet and put it back on the cover of the Book, but it wouldn't lock back into place. I got frustrated with my inability, but as if in response to my aggravation, the amulet lit up and that strange humming happened again. A flood of green light filled the room." Opa gestured around the room as if to recreate that feeling.

"I know exactly what you are talking about," I said excitedly. "That is what happened to me just now with the amulet—the bright green light and the humming sound!"

"I've seen and experienced many things on my journeys, but I have never come across such raw power in my life. The stone necklace I wear is nothing compared to the power of this amulet. For me, I have had to read the Book to gain its meaning, but with your amulet, you are directly linked to its knowledge and power. As Soljourners, we have only encountered fractions of the Book's real potential, but you will be something greater. You will become a part of the Book," Opa said as he looked at me with awe.

I suddenly had a thought. "I could probably find my mom and dad by wearing the amulet and then asking the Book where they are!"

Opa looked surprised and said, "We need to make sure you have the willpower to keep yourself separated from the Book. Otherwise, you could easily be consumed by its power."

"Why is that a problem? Why can't I? If I have such power to make a difference in the world, then why not try?"

"Your father wanted to make a more significant impact too, and he strayed from his path. If you choose the same for yourself, it could potentially cost you not only your life but the lives of many others around you. The time that governs Earth is not the same as time itself. Time is a living entity. It has a consciousness; it is neutral to all things, including the light and the dark. So, the closer you are to the Emerald Book, the more aligned you are with real-time and not Earth's time."

"But what if I have the power to bring about world peace or solve illness and starvation?"

"That would be amazing and wonderful, but what are the greater consequences of doing such an act when it's also acting out against others' free will? You're forcing them into a reality that you want to create without them having the choice to do it."

I felt my impatience growing; I felt the pull of the amulet towards me and the energy building inside of me; I felt a tug of war between peace and power—the desire for the amulet and the intensity of so many other emotions fighting each other within me.

"Are you okay?" asked Opa.

"No, I'm frustrated."

"Well, it's through our own choices that we either feed the light or the dark. But it's only through the masses that we can bring about change that's good for all of us. Within ourselves, we have a lightness and darkness that are equal to everyone else's, but it's free will that separates everybody's realities. That's a cosmic law. The idea of global peace is virtually impossible until each of us can accept our own shadow without feeling the need to destroy it."

"You say it starts with one person, one reality . . . well, I want to make a difference," I told him determinedly.

"Your missions are how you will make a difference, win or lose. Even in our comic books, there is constant conflict."

"Then at least let me try."

"Orabella, our missions are set. We can't just simply change the rules."

"The Soljourners are capable of so much more, but we're confined to rules. Why can't we change them?" I protested.

"It doesn't work that way. Our guidelines are precise. The shoes help us go back to the exact spot we must be in to keep history progressing. Certain things in life must happen!" Opa exclaimed.

"But why? What if I could go back in time and help people like Princess Diana? Michael Jackson? Warn them of their unfortunate fates? There's so much good we can do."

"Ah, I'm happy you're thinking this through, but remember, we cannot just interfere with people's lives. It's our free will to accept the consequences of what has happened by not doing it in our own lives."

If we had such a powerful weapon as the knowledge of the universe at our disposal, then why couldn't we make a bigger difference? I began to understand where my dad was coming from, but then again, I felt that I may have gotten him and my mom in trouble. I felt a change was coming in how things had been done for so long. A new way of doing these missions was possible, but it seemed pointless to talk to Opa about it. I needed to work with Wadjet more, and for the first time in my life, I was looking forward to going to bed so I could work with her in Dreamtime.

"I'm exhausted. I think I'll head off to bed," I said.

"Really? It's only 8 PM. Are you feeling okay?" Opa asked with concern.

"Yes, it's been a long day. Good night, Opa."

"You're not going to sleep here? It will be safer," Opa said, motioning to the pull-out bed.

"No, I feel more comfortable in the house—in my bed," I said.

As I walked up the spiral staircase and back through the work area, I noticed I felt much less powerful than I had next to the strength of the Book and the amulet. I could feel some of my fear and anxiety returning. *Oh, how frustrating. Maybe I should sneak back later and take the amulet.* I ran into the house, straight up to my bedroom. I picked up Lolo, who was waiting on top of my bed for me.

I was way too tired to put on pyjamas, so I flopped onto my sheets. I heard Scarlett in my head telling me one of her puns. "The future, the present, and the past walked into a bar. Things got a little tense." How appropriate that I would remember that one.

15

FAIRY FISHING—JULY 7TH, 5:45 AM

"Orabella, wake up," Opa said, nudging me.

"What is it? It looks dark out still," I mumbled tiredly.

"It's very early. Get dressed. We're taking a day off. We're going fishing."

"What? Okay, I'm up, just give me a few minutes to wash my face and brush my teeth," I said groggily.

"Hurry up. I made breakfast. We'll eat on the way,"

I slowly rolled out of bed and changed my clothes before going into the bathroom. I stared, unenthused, at my reflection in the mirror as I brushed my teeth, and I saw a glimmer of green flash in my eyes. Seeing this magical flash gave me a burst of energy I didn't think was possible at this hour. I knew what happened yesterday with Wadjet was not a dream. I spat out my toothpaste and leapt down the stairs excitedly but also quietly so I wouldn't wake Oma.

I ran into Opa in the kitchen.

"Did you do any Dreamtime work with Wadjet last night?"

"No, I slept so deeply I had no dreams at all."

"I guess you got a day off. Grab a breakfast sandwich and one of my hats on the coat rack just in case the mosquitos are biting."

"Oh, yuck. I forgot about that," I replied.

We ate our egg and bacon croissants in the car while we drove to the fishing spot.

"Not sure how many we'll catch, but it's worth a try. A break from routine. I know you've only been with us for a bit, but you've learned a lot in a very short amount of time."

I looked out the window of the truck. I could see the faint glow of the sunrise, which reminded me of the day that I came here. *Wow, so much has happened since that day.*

"I have a boat moored at a lake up the coast. It will only take a few minutes to get there."

I only nodded my head in agreement as I looked out and thought about all that had happened and how my life had changed forever. Less than two weeks ago, I was getting ready to go to high school. Yes, I was feeling uncertain about it, but that uncertainty was nothing compared to this. How would I explain any of this to my friends?

Oh, hi, girls, how was your summer? Well, my mom and dad vanished into thin air, and it turns out there is a big family secret. I'm the last of the Soljourners! We protect the Tree of Life from an evil genie. I was given an amulet that gives me powers, and I have goddesses as friends, who look like all of you, but don't worry, they could never replace you. Oh, and I have to stop the evil genie from going back in time and changing history. Otherwise, the world will come to an end!

Sincerely, Bella.

I smiled as I composed this letter in my head. I knew I would never be able to explain it to anyone.

Opa looked over at me. "If your mom and dad could reach out to us, they would. They are okay. I can feel it. They're strong. In many ways, your mom could have easily been a Soljourner herself. Since she used to be a history teacher, very much like Oma, she would help your dad prepare for missions by researching time periods and locations. Then, when your mom decided to change professions, she became an advocate for artists, helping to nourish the Tree of Life by bringing the standard and respectability of artists to the same level as any professional. Your father was the sidekick."

Both of us laughed.

"I wouldn't say you are more like your mother or your father. You have always been courageous and willing to try new things—much like the two of them. Throughout our long history, missions have been very lonely, as we didn't want to burden our partners with what happened when we returned from them. Like soldiers returning from the war, we kept it to ourselves, but your mom and dad made a good team, and your Oma has always done her best to try to understand the worries and stress I have been put under in my search for Iblis. Luckily, while we are away, time slows or completely stops, so our family hardly notices our absence, but there is an emotional toll that the missions take on us."

I sat there quietly and listened to all that Opa had to say. There were so many things I hadn't taken into consideration.

"Your father is also the first in our long history to not take up any sort of profession in shoes. Instead, he opened a hat store, which initially made me very unhappy. I felt that he was breaking from tradition and that, somehow, he would be punished for it. We didn't speak for many years. It was your mother who kept us in the loop. They were aware of your destiny when you were born; they knew that your path would be far different from the rest.

"My father, your Great-Opa, was a stubborn believer in trial-by-error. I am amazed that I passed my first journey alive. It made me stronger, but because of that, I ensured my son was prepared. Your father resisted, much like yourself, and felt that his path was different. Once he got older, things changed. He rebelled. He didn't want anything to do with it. He was much older when the forces of destiny pushed against him, and he couldn't resist anymore.

"That is the delicate balance between our free will and destiny. We may have our plans and often blame the universe and even the gods themselves for our failures, but all too often, it's because we are on the wrong path. When the way becomes apparent, we often resist it because we're scared. We all live by universal principles that keep everything in balance."

The more time I spend in the Shoe Chamber, the more I feel I can absorb everything that Opa says, I thought to myself, but there was something else growing inside me—a feeling I'd never had before . . . Was it confidence?

"Opa, could I meet you or Dad when you were younger on one of my missions?" I blurted out with enthusiasm.

"Yes, that's a possibility, but again, you can't identify yourself or interfere. Time is fickle, and we don't want to create a time curve. That's why shoes are so important. They have the DNA of where exactly in history you're going, both place and time."

Opa stopped talking when we arrived at the lake; there was nobody there, and the solitude was eerie—almost too quiet. As Opa and I loaded up the boat, I thought again about how it was still so hard to comprehend most of what I had been told, but I felt that as soon as I could grasp it, I could make a difference in the world.

"Orabella, stop daydreaming. I need your help getting the boat to the pond."

I snapped out of my reverie and got into the boat, using one of the oars to push against the bank and get some movement. Then, Opa jumped in at the back of the boat. We slowly rowed out to the middle of the lake and loaded up our lure with the juiciest of worms. It was freezing out on the lake in the early morning, but I tried not to show Opa that I was uncomfortable. We both threw our lines out on opposite sides of the boat. Several minutes went by, and not a bite. I quickly got impatient.

Opa leaned back against me and said, "Take a deep breath and wiggle your toes."

I closed my eyes and did as he instructed.

"When we get to that point in our thoughts where we feel anxious, we need to slow our minds down with our breathing," Opa explained. "If we get impatient or bored because we want a result to happen based on an expectation, focusing on our breath allows us to focus on the moment. By being in the moment, we become the observer and not the doer."

I remembered my dream where I floated amidst the chaos. If I could be calm then, I certainly could be calm now at this moment.

As I closed my eyes and felt my chest expand and collapse with my breath, I felt the rod between my hands. I sensed the warmth of my breath. I heard the silence around me. I began to drift peacefully as if I were floating, and the only thing that mattered was my breathing. I then felt a tug on my line. *A bite!* I got excited and pulled back against it, but in my haste, I lost it.

Opa turned around. "You almost got it. It's with your silence that the fish feel safe enough to approach your line. Especially now, when nature is so quiet. By letting go of expectations, you let go of where and how you ended up there."

The sun had come up above us, and I kept trying to relinquish my thoughts back to that place, but far more distractions were around me, making it harder to focus. The birds were waking up, and so were the mosquitoes. Opa, in his silence, caught two fish, which annoyed me. Yes, I was comparing myself to him, but it was hard not to. My head became so full of chattering thoughts I didn't know where to begin. I was struggling.

I suddenly heard Opa take a deep breath, which reminded me that breathing was so easy to forget. We took for granted that we breathe every day. I was finally able to get back to that place of peaceful mindfulness, and I felt myself falling into that position again, that calmness. Again, my line tugged, but this time I didn't pull. I took my time, and with each breath, I reeled in my line slowly and steadily.

But when I looked out over the side of the boat to look at my catch, I didn't see a fish but a human face looking up at me. It looked like my friend, Remi. *What the heck?* I stood up and yanked on Opa's coat to get his attention. I almost forgot I was in a boat and nearly toppled us both overboard to my surprise. As I steadied myself, I watched Remi float up out of the water like a ghost. She looked so young. Her skin was pale, and her eyes were the deepest blue I had ever seen. Her hair was straight down to her knees, wispy and blonde. She looked to be four feet tall and delicate like a sheet. She wore a dress that was as white as her skin and her hair. Even though she had come from the water, she did not appear to be wet at all. Opa and I stared at her speechlessly.

"Hello, I'm Aine—a fairy goddess—and I've come to introduce myself to you," the delicate being said with a giggle. Maybe it was because we looked so scared.

"Oh, hello, Aine, awesome to meet you. Are you like the queen of the fairies?" The real Remi would have freaked out knowing that a fairy goddess looked like her. She loved fairy lore.

"Yes, I'm of the dimension where many of your legends and stories of fairies come from," Aine said.

"Like Tinkerbell?"

"Yes, that's the idea!" Her voice rang out clear across the glassy lake. Then, she raised her hands, and out of the trees and bushes, a few hundred tiny people flew out around the lake. They looked more like winged ghosts floating across the water. You could see through their pale skin as they circled us. I could hear their wings beat against the wind as they flew. It sounded like the wings of a thousand hummingbirds. Opa was quiet, and so was I. All I could do was smile like I was a little child all over again. It was so beautiful and magical. Aine lowered her arms, and they were gone, back to the forest. Only she remained floating in front of us.

"We, from the fairy realm, are here to assist you on your journey. We will be meeting with you very soon to reveal your special gift. Your transition is coming. Do not be afraid of the darkness."

Before I could ask her any questions, she disappeared back into the water. I turned to Opa, who had his mouth wide open in silence.

"Opa, have you met Aine before?"

Opa blinked his eyes a few times before he spoke. "No, I haven't. It seems you have many on your side to help you. I've never had so many unexpected visitors."

"Many of them have told me that they would meet me after this transition . . . do you know what they are talking about?"

"I think it has something to do with your birthday. You'll be thirteen soon—officially a teenager!"

"You think it's all because of my birthday?"

Opa nodded his head and we quietly rowed back ashore. We tied down the boat and loaded the truck back up. While Opa cleaned his fish, I looked to see if I could spot some more fairies, or even Aine, but the only thing that I found was mosquitoes.

Opa put his hands on my shoulders. "You continue to surprise me."

"What do you mean?"

"Well, with Aine showing up today and Wadjet, Morrigan, and Liberty appearing the last few days, it shows you are destined for something greater than I ever could have imagined. All I can say is hang on to who you are, regardless of all of this attention."

"Okay, Opa, I will," I said as I hugged him. "Can we skip some rocks off the water before we go?"

"We sure can, kiddo. I haven't done that in a long time."

We searched along the ground to find the flattest rocks, and Opa and I took turns skipping stones along the lake water. The sun was shining, and I felt happy—like I was close to going home where I belonged. The doubt within myself had disappeared.

We got into the truck and started to drive down the bumpy dirt path to the main road. I rolled up my window as a cloud of dust flew into the truck, and I started to cough. As we arrived at the main road, there was a sign neither of us had noticed on our way in. It was a development notice that there would be a resort built around the lake, and that a private walk-on ferry service would be provided for the guests of the resort. The lake would become off-limits to the very residents that currently lived on the lake. I was shocked and mad. Opa was surprised.

"How can they do that? How can someone just buy a lake?" I asked indignantly.

"If it's on private land or land sold commercially, there's nothing we can do about it but protest through the local mayor's office," Opa replied dejectedly.

"Does that mean we can't fish here anymore?" I demanded. I loved the peacefulness of the practice, not the actual fishing part of it.

Opa looked sad and replied, "Yes, but it also means that we'll have to find another lake to fish out of. Life is about change, and with change comes an opportunity to grow and explore something new. There are times we need to fight for what is right. I will speak with Oma about this and see what we can do. But in most cases, the decisions have already been made for us."

"That isn't fair. Those developers didn't ask us what we thought."

"Well, most of the time there are public consultations and forums where the community can gather and speak about it, but sometimes, when there is enough money and influence, that gets bypassed. Yes, it's unfair, but again, it's another distraction that creates more divisions among us. Now the lake will not be shared by the owner."

"Oh, that makes me so mad, Opa. How can people be so selfish?" It struck me that I now knew the difference between the times when Opa had the necklace and when he didn't. When he had it with him, he was wiser, more grounded, and way more talkative. I giggled to myself and decided to ask.

"Do you have the stone with you?"

Opa looked over at me and grinned. "Yes, I do. Why do you ask?"

"Just curious," I said as I grinned back at him. *I can't wait to get the amulet back to feel its power inside me*. What were the special gift and transition Aine mentioned? Was it because of my connection to the amulet? I also felt like I was getting closer to finding Mom and Dad. I didn't feel scared anymore. I no longer feared being alone.

16

PIE FACE—JULY 7TH, 11:30 AM

We arrived back home, and it was perfect timing for brunch. Oma waved to us from the porch as we drove in. Opa always had a smile on his face whenever Oma was around. It was so sweet to see real love. I hadn't experienced it myself and I was not ready for it, especially with everything going on, but one day I hoped to find the same love that Opa and Oma had.

As we approached, Oma called out to us, "Lunch is ready! Did you catch any fish for dinner?"

"Yes, we caught three of them. Orabella is a natural! She even caught a fairy queen!"

"You caught what? Did I hear that right?" she asked.

"We got more than we expected from fishing," Opa told her.

"Wow!" Oma said with a stunned expression, still surprised by everything that came with Opa's world.

"She mentioned something about a 'special gift' I have," I said.

We were all quiet as Oma looked to Opa for an answer, but he shrugged his shoulders. Oma looked concerned.

"Oh, also there is a new development going on at the lake. Looks like we'll be cut off from the fishing spot."

"Oh no, that's terrible. This is the first I'm hearing of it," Oma remarked sadly.

"Well, let's sit down for lunch, and we'll fill you in on our adventure," Opa said.

During lunch, Opa chatted with Oma about the lake development, which made Oma angry. "This is unacceptable. We need to speak with the town council as to why this is being allowed."

"I agree that this is not fair," Opa said.

"Well, it also appears that we have new neighbours next door," Oma announced.

"Oh, that didn't take very long. The property was on the market for only a couple of weeks. Yes, it seems like the whole city wants to move here," Opa said.

"I did notice that they have a girl that looks to be Bella's age. They look familiar, but I couldn't place them. Maybe after lunch, you can take over a pie to welcome the new neighbours? Perhaps you'll make a friend," Oma suggested to me.

Opa and I looked at each other, and I was sure we were thinking the same thing: I had way too much training to do to go meet new neighbours, but after I finished helping with the dishes, Oma handed me a homemade blackberry pie and I made my way over to the property next door. I noticed the moving vans out front unloading the furniture, and I saw a girl run into the house.

Seeing someone my age got me excited. *Somebody to hang out with!* There had been so much to do around the farm and so much learning with Opa that there hadn't been time to make friends in the community. It would be helpful to have a friend to play games and do crafts with, maybe even have a teen vlog if I could make the time. I hoped they weren't living off the grid-like us. *Oma will freak out if they have internet*. I giggled at the thought.

I walked into the driveway and headed straight to the house, which was more modern than Oma's house, but had less land. I got to the door and knocked. While I waited for someone to answer, I could hear voices talking on the other side. There was something about one of the voices that sounded familiar. Suddenly, I placed the voice, and a giant brick dropped into my stomach that ached beyond belief. The door opened, my eyes widened, and I dropped the pie all over my feet.

"Hello there, neighbour," said Rachelle with her jet black hair and snide voice.

I couldn't believe it! Of all the people in the world, why did it have to be *her?*

"*So* looking forward to living beside you," she sneered with a twisted grin.

My breath was caught in my chest. I stood there motionless, not even able to pick up the mess at my feet.

"Oh, you dummy, you dropped the pie. What is wrong with you?"

I heard her mother in the background, but all I wanted to do was run. We both stood there for a moment, and I could feel the same terror and shame now that she had always tried to lay on me at school.

"What? How? Why did you move here?" I stammered in disbelief.

She folded her arms and leaned forward to get right in my face. "Because I missed scaring you," she replied and laughed.

Compared to yesterday, I felt like a loser. How could Rachelle trigger me? How could I feel so powerless after everything I had learned? I felt angry with myself.

"No, really, I did, but my dad is also the owner of the lake near here and is building some sort of resort. We have to live here until it's built."

I was shocked and almost screamed at her but held back. "What? Your dad is the one who's cutting off the lake?"

"Oh yeah, Orabella. He's building a huge resort and bringing lots of rich people to this horrible, boring place. He noticed the listing for the land at the local real estate agent the day we saw you at the market. My dad knows everybody. He wanted all the land around the lake, so he called a few people in the government and got what he wanted. So, my only joy of being here is to make your life miserable. Seriously, Orabella, you thought that by coming here, you would get me out of your life? Well, you can't always get what you want, even if your parents do go missing mysteriously."

How does she know about my parents? How can she speak to me this way? It was all so cruel.

"So, go run back to your old grandparents, because I will be watching you, and my mom will be over to meet your grandparents so we can become *terrific* friends," she said with the most despicable falsity in her voice. "Now go and leave me alone. But you better clean up this pie before you leave. You're so messy."

Her mom arrived at the door wearing almost the same style of clothing as Rachelle, and her black hair was also styled similarly. Rachelle's mom always seemed so polite and confident, while her daughter was so mean. Rachelle reached down to pick up the pie that had fallen out of my hand.

"Hi, Mom. Sorry for the mess, but you remember my friend, Orabella, from school in the city. She's our new neighbour. She stopped by with a pie for us, but she dropped it all over the front doorstep. Don't worry, I am helping her with it."

Rachelle's mom said, "Oh, Rachelle, you're a great help. Orabella, you really should be more careful."

My cheeks turned bright red. Without any of the Girl Squad here to back me up, I was completely alone against Rachelle.

Rachelle said with a smirk and a wink, "I guess Orabella will have to bring us another welcome-to-the-neighbourhood pie."

I stared at her in utter shock. Her eyes were completely black like Theom's had been the night of the solstice. Dark and filled with hatred and anger. I could feel myself quake with fear, and I questioned my worth as a superhero who was destined to save the world when I couldn't even stand up to one girl my age.

I bent down to pick up the pie off the floor when Rachelle slammed the door in my face. I could hear her tell her mom that it was the wind that blew it closed.

I couldn't believe what had just happened. I slowly walked back to the house, feeling numb. When I got there, I went into the kitchen where Oma was standing. She watched me silently as I came in, and I couldn't stop myself from bursting into tears. She ran to me and held me tightly. Oma led me over to the chair and I told her the whole story.

"Well, we'll have to do something about that."

"No, Oma. I don't want to be friends with her. I need to learn how to stand up for myself and not feel like a complete idiot around her," I replied defeatedly.

"So, do you feel like she steals your strength and power away from you?"

"Yes, and I get angry with myself because I don't know how to stop it."

"Orabella, we're going to have to work on that in your training so nobody can take your power away," she said with a determined face.

"Thank you, Oma. I just can't believe how I could feel so powerful yesterday and so weak today," I said feebly.

"Remember the black wolf and white wolf story?" Oma asked. "That's natural. Some people trigger us, so we must train ourselves not to be bothered by their words. It's how we keep the white wolf strong within us; it's how we learn to not let that happen." She patted my arm reassuringly.

"My mind goes blank when I'm around her," I said.

"Tomorrow is a new day. I will give you exercises to practice," Oma said.

I gave Oma a big hug. "I love you, Oma. Thank you."

"I love you too, Bella. Now go for a walk to clear your mind—maybe down by the stream."

"Okay, good idea. Thank you, Oma." I smiled at her and stood up from my chair.

I walked out past the tree to the stream and down to the swinging tire. I noticed that, yet again, Lolo was stretched out under the tree. She didn't even move when she saw me.

"Wow, to have a cat's life," I murmured to myself with a chuckle as I passed by her.

I was swinging from the tire, and with each swing, I could hear the wind rustling through the trees and the water rushing by. It was nature's music. I enjoyed listening to it, but suddenly, it was interrupted by the clanging of a tone-deaf voice.

"Well, hi there, neighbour. So, I forgot to ask—what school will you be going to?"

I was initially startled but quickly told myself to remain calm. I smiled back and said, "I'm not. I'm being homeschooled by my Oma, and we're having international students coming in to help me learn languages, so I'll have new friends abroad."

Oh boy, she did not look happy to hear that. Her smile quickly turned upside down.

She scowled at me. "Well, then, I'll have to find other ways to make your life miserable here. Oh, by the way, can I join you on the tire swing—*my* tire swing?"

"What are you talking about? The tire swing is on our land."

Rachelle laughed. "Well, actually, it's not. The tree and tire are on our part of the property line, according to my dad and his lawyer, so get off my swing now!"

Once again, I could not control my emotions while being around her. "Really? You want to fight over a swinging tire?"

"There's nothing to fight over. This is my tire, and I'm telling you you're on my land, so get off it now! Go home to your old grandparents. These are my rules now, so get off!"

I got off the swing and jumped back over to the opposite side of the creek from where she was standing. I stared at her in anger and disbelief.

"So, unless you get permission from me, don't get on this tire again or even climb this tree. It's mine—all mine. Now go home and cry. Go, cry like a baby. You're so sensitive."

I just stood there, feeling like a punching bag. Rachelle was a terrible person and just kept getting worse.

"My dad is also looking at buying the property behind you, too, so no crossing the creek when he buys it."

I looked at her, seeing the rage behind her grin, and asked her, "Rachelle, why are you so lonely and in so much pain that you feel the need to hurt others?"

Her mouth dropped open. She was speechless for a moment but quickly recovered. "Listen, dummy, you don't know what you're talking about, and soon I'll be all around you. You'll have nowhere to go."

I laughed out loud. "Well, you have no idea. I don't even need to leave the property, and I can go anywhere I want."

I realized I had said too much. She looked at me curiously, and then said in a weird voice that sounded much different from her usual mocking tone, "I knew we would finally find you."

The way she said it made my hair stand up on end. *What does that mean?*

I backed away from her slowly then turned around and ran to the house. *What did she mean?* As the air rushed past me, my fear lessened, and my pride swelled. *I finally stood up to Rachelle!* I felt her power over me lessening. My run slowed to a walk as I neared the house with a newfound sense of freedom inside of me. I smelled dinner coming from the kitchen and realized I should go help set the table.

It suddenly hit me: the dream of me falling into the abyss was a lesson. It taught me to stay present with the amulet and now with Rachelle. Each time I stopped breathing in fear, my emotions and body were not in my control. But when I let go and breathed through it, I could get through these trials successfully. *Yes!* I screamed out in my head and jumped up in the air. I would have to tell Oma and Opa about these successes. As I slowly walked towards the back of the house, I felt my love and appreciation for my family swell. I loved Oma, Opa, and Lolo so much.

I decided to make a detour to Opa's workhouse to look for him before I went to the kitchen to help Oma. When I opened the door, I was surprised to see Wadjet there in the workshop, guarding the entrance to the stairwell.

"Hello, Orabella. Let us continue our training with the amulet."

I nodded at her in agreement.

"To be safe, we need to go into Dreamtime, so the amulet does not take over your body."

"What exactly is Dreamtime?"

"Well, Dreamtime is like your dreams, but you are completely aware of what is happening. You are aware that you are sleeping, so your fears do not limit you in your experience there."

"Is it safe there?"

"Yes, it is. Dreamtime is secure with anybody you invite into it. It's a place where dreams exist like rooms with no doors. And with Lolo here to guard your body in the Shoe Chamber, no one will be able to harm you while we practice."

We headed down the spiral staircase and opened the door to the Chamber. Wadjet floated across the room and directed me towards the couch. "Please lie down," she said.

I noticed she had the amulet in her hand.

"I am going to ask you to go to sleep."

"But I'm not tired."

"I am going to leave and allow you to relax. Once I feel your body and mind are relaxed, I will slip you into Dreamtime." Wadjet's voice became calming and melodic.

I stifled a yawn. "Okay," I said as I sat down on the couch.

Wadjet left, and in the back of my mind, I felt uneasy that she had taken the amulet with her. Even though she was its creator, I felt that it belonged to me now. I pushed those thoughts aside as sleep seemed much more delightful than worry. The Shoe Chamber was quiet, and soon it disappeared around me as I drifted into Dreamtime without even trying.

"That didn't take you long," Wadjet remarked as she stood by the Tree of Life with the amulet in her hand.

"Why did we have to meet here?

"I feel stronger here than at your home. Besides, this is a much more beautiful setting, being here at the centre of the universe." Wadjet opened her hand and, to my surprise, the amulet floated out of it. It aimed directly at my chest. It attached itself to me, and I felt its power surge into me. I began to hyperventilate.

"Orabella, you need to breathe into the amulet," Wadjet said.

"I'm trying, but its power is stronger here in Dreamtime. And when I close my eyes, I see myself back in the Shoe Chamber sleeping. It's so weird to be in two places at once."

"Impressive, Orabella, that you can stay conscious in your dreams. With practice, you will be able to investigate your dreams while you are awake and look into any dimension from the moment you are in Dreamtime," Wadjet said.

I thought of what Opa told me about the apartment analogy. Instead of going between floors, I could now see everything that was going on from the outside. *Cool.*

"But do not be distracted by your feelings, Orabella. You are a very passionate human, but your intense feelings can cloud your judgment, and that can get you into trouble."

I felt the pulse of the amulet against my chest. I loved this connection. I loved its power.

"So, what is the buzzing I hear and the pulse I feel?" I asked.

"You are connected to the amulet, which is connected to the Emerald Tablet, which is connected to the Tree of Life. The buzz you hear is the first sound of life, and the pulse is the heartbeat of the universe. You are tapped into all of creation."

"If I can imagine it, I can create it? Like flying?" I said enthusiastically.

"Yes, the power of the amulet is limitless; however, the greatness of its power is the reason why we have hidden it for so long. You must be careful in how you use it."

"If I have so much power, then why do I need the goddesses' powers to aid me in my journeys?"

"Even though you have unlimited power with the amulet, you will still need assistance from each of the goddesses. They are directly connected to the cultural experiences you will have."

"Then why do I need to be homeschooled? Why do I need to travel and learn if I have this universal knowledge?"

"You still need to be prepared with the knowledge that experience brings," Wadjet said confidently. "You can't only depend on the amulet. You should be able to have the confidence, knowledge, and power within you, and this will be reflected in the power you get from the amulet. The more knowledge you gain for yourself, the more you will get from the amulet. But never think you can do this alone. The goddesses and I are here to assist you."

"So, you're saying that as I learn and grow and go on these missions, the knowledge that is bestowed upon me is accumulated into the amulet?" I asked.

"Yes, and over time, you will be able to pull from the amulet what you gained from each experience at any time without the assistance of that specific goddess," Wadjet responded.

"So, it's sort of like I have zero energy, and when I go on these missions, I gain power points to charge up my amulet, like in a video game."

"I do not know much about video games, but I do know that you must first be able to control the power of the amulet, which is about being clear with your emotions. Humans are compelled by their emotions. It drives them to create or destroy, and with their capacity for free will, it can create a lot of chaos."

"Yes, my mom always says you can't meet anger with anger. Nobody wins that way, and you must have the courage and strength to walk away from situations that can hurt you more," I said.

"That is very insightful. Be mindful of your feelings. Stay focused on the present moment and breathe. I think now is a good time to end our session."

Before I knew it, I was back on the couch in the Shoe Chamber with Lolo lying next to me. Lolo felt my body jolt as I woke up in the physical realm, and she looked up at me and meowed. She seemed agitated.

Lolo meowed again, and I noticed the amulet was back on the Book.

I gave her a couple of strokes to the back of her neck, and she automatically began to purr. I was so excited. I really needed to tell somebody. *Who should I explain this to first? Scarlett, Alexa, Olivia, Georgia, or Camille?*

As I was thinking about my friends and who to tell, I heard in my head, "Breathe. Control your emotions. Remember the outcome of your actions."

Right, this was supposed to be a secret. I couldn't tell anybody. Total bummer, which reminded me I still needed to get a charger, but I was so distracted all the time. I kept forgetting. Maybe that was a good thing right now, not having a phone, or else I might have made a mistake by telling somebody.

With all these lessons, I was losing track of time and what day it was. I also felt that my new role as a Soljourner would feel more meaningful if I had a cool outfit to wear for these adventures, like a superhero cape or costume. I got up from the couch and walked over to the desk to find a piece of paper and a pencil. Would I wear a cape? Would I look good in a cape? *What is the purpose of a cape anyway? Don't they just get in the way? I would love to be able to fly, and technically I would be flying through time. How cool is that? Every superhero needs a costume.* It was so weird thinking of myself as a hero. I started to giggle uncontrollably. *Yeah, a superhero that needs to go to the bathroom every time she gets nervous.*

But what kind of colours would I like on my outfit? I started doing designs for my costume. I wasn't big on capes and dresses, so something practical—maybe pants with a long flowing shirt. Before I knew it, the wastebasket was full of failed attempts, but I felt like I was getting closer. I sat back and thought about all the comic book heroes I loved and which costumes I liked the best.

While I sat there contemplating my outfit, I noticed the lights dim and the temperature drop. I got goosebumps all over my body. I began to see my breath as a cloud streaming from my nostrils. The darkness felt thick like a fog. My heart was racing. *Oh, no! Is it Iblis?* I jumped up and grabbed the amulet. My heart was pounding. I felt the energy of the amulet pulsing in my hand. In the corner of the room, by the old leather chairs, a black figure appeared out of the dark, grey fog. I was ready.

17

ACCIDENTS HAPPEN—JULY 8TH, 9:20 AM

"Hello, child. How is your training going with Wadjet?" Morrigan asked ominously as she floated out of the shadows towards me.

"Don't scare me like that! Please be less dramatic next time. But to answer your question, the training is going well," I replied, thinking that I didn't want to share too much with her. But then again, she seemed to know what was happening already.

"So, are you feeling more comfortable with the amulet, my child?"

"Can you please call me Orabella? Also, can you please be less creepy? Yes, I feel more connected to the amulet."

"That is good because you will soon need it. A great challenge is about to happen in your life."

"What challenge? And how do you know this?"

I felt myself losing control of my emotions again. I felt scared. I told myself to breathe, to keep calm, and to hold my tongue around Morrigan.

"Why are you here?"

"I've come because death is near. Safe passage is needed for the soul," Morrigan replied with a smile on her lips.

"What do you mean? Don't scare me like that," I replied, feeling myself losing control and starting to panic.

My head began to ring, and I felt a huge knot in my stomach. Something had happened. I got the same vision I had before of Opa in an accident. My stomach was turning, and I ran up the spiral staircase and out of the workshop as quickly as possible.

I heard a loud screech of tires. I looked towards the road. I was frozen and couldn't turn away.

"Opa!" I cried out. This couldn't be happening. I turned around to yell at Morrigan to help, but she was gone.

Like watching a movie in slow motion, I could see Opa's truck flip over in midair and disappear into the ditch on the other side of the road. A loud explosion buffeted my ears as his car landed at the bottom.

I felt the blood rushing in my ears. I cried out, "No! Opa!"

I heard the front door slam and saw Oma running out to the street. I couldn't move, but it seemed like Oma was running in slow motion.

"Call 911!" she called to me as she ran. But instead of moving, I caught something in the corner of my eye that held me in place a moment longer. I saw the reflection of black hair glistening in the sunlight. My attention darted over to the road, and there I could see Rachelle walking off the highway with her back to the house. *What is she doing on the road?*

I broke free of my paralysis and ran into the house to call 911. My hands were shaking as I dialed each number. It felt like it took forever. There was a ringing in the receiver, but nobody was picking up. Finally, there was a click.

"911 Emergency. Do you require fire, police, or ambulance?" the dispatcher asked curtly.

"All of them! Please, my Opa's truck flipped over. There was a crash, and I see a small fire!"

"What is your address?"

My mind was blank. I kept thinking of my address back in Vancouver. I looked around for a bill and spotted the electric bill on the counter.

"It's 2489 Lockyear. Please, hurry!"

"That's 2489 Lockyear Road," the dispatcher replied calmly.

"Yes, please hurry!" I yelled.

I ran out of the door, up the driveway and onto the highway. I saw Oma trying to open Opa's door to pull him out. Smoke billowed from the small fire at the front of the truck.

"Oma! I called 911. They're coming!"

"Thank you. See if we can find a way to get him out. I think he's passed out." Oma was shaken. Her instructions were robotic. She was in shock.

We both screamed out to Opa as we banged on the window.

"Wake up, Opa!" I cried.

I heard hissing and pulled away from the truck. "Oma, the fire is getting bigger!"

"Try to find something to break the window!" Oma yelled back.

Oma didn't hear me and kept trying to yank on the truck door handle to get Opa out of the wreckage. I heard sirens off in the distance. *Why are they taking so long?* It seemed like forever. We were frantic. I saw Oma trying to smash open the driver's window with a large stick. I heard the sirens getting closer, but it wasn't fast enough. As I looked around, I saw Rachelle on the other side of the street from her driveway. I saw her mom rushing out of the house. Rachelle had a big smile on her face, which made me so angry that I wanted to run across the street and tear her head off.

Oma kept banging away at the car window, but it wasn't cracking. There was smoke coming out of the passenger side of the engine. I was afraid that the truck would blow up.

I heard Rachelle's mom call out as she rushed up to me. "I've called 911! How can we help?"

I was so angry that I yelled at her, "This is Rachelle's fault! I saw her on the highway from when the truck crashed!"

Rachelle's mom looked at me, confused. "Rachelle was with me in the kitchen baking cookies when we heard the crash. She ran out to the road first while I called 911. I'm sorry about the accident, but don't blame my daughter."

Rachelle's mom turned around and walked back to the other side of the road to stand with Rachelle, who was not smiling anymore. I was livid. I knew what I saw. Why was her mom lying to cover for her?

The fire truck arrived first. The ambulance soon followed, and finally, the police. One firefighter pulled Oma away from the truck while another broke the driver's side window. Another firefighter put out the fire with a large extinguisher.

One of the ambulance drivers walked over to us. "Are you both okay? Were you involved in the accident?"

"No. We both saw it from the house," I said as I pointed to our house.

"I heard it from my kitchen," Oma said with tears pouring down her face. She stared at the truck as she spoke.

The firefighters finally removed Opa from the truck. And just as they pulled him out of the window, a raven flew down and landed onto the overturned truck. Was that Morrigan? I suddenly remembered my vision of the accident. I knew this was going to happen, but I didn't pay attention to it. I started to cry. I could have prevented this from happening if I had only listened.

The firefighters transferred Opa onto a stretcher. His head was bleeding, and he wasn't moving. We both rushed towards him, but two police officers and a fireman held us back. Opa was put into the ambulance and rushed off.

Oma and I were crying, and she kept saying, "Jasper, you're tough and stubborn—fight this!"

A police officer who was attempting to restrain us started to ask questions. "Are you related to the person involved in the accident?"

"Yes, I'm his wife, and this is his granddaughter," Oma said. All I could do was nod my head. Had anyone else seen Rachelle at the scene of the accident?

The officer looked at Oma. "Did you see what happened?"

"Not exactly, officer, I was in my kitchen making lunch when I heard a loud crash." Oma pointed towards the house.

"And what did you see?" The officer directed his question at me.

"I heard tires screeching. Then the truck flipped, and then a loud bang. I also saw that girl on the road," I said as I pointed to Rachelle, who was still across the street with her mom.

"Did you notice anything else?" the officer asked Oma.

"I only heard the tires and the explosion. Then I ran out of the house to see what was happening," Oma replied softly.

"Ma'am, did you notice the girl across the street?"

"I'm sorry, I didn't. I was running for the truck so fast that I don't think I even checked for traffic when I ran across the road," Oma admitted.

I felt blood rushing to my face. I felt embarrassed and angry that no one believed me.

The officer looked at me again. "So, you're sure you saw that girl on the road when the truck flipped?"

"Yes!"

"Okay, I need to go speak with her and her mom," he said and walked away from us towards Rachelle.

"Oma, I know what I saw," I said defensively as she cried silently.

"We don't have a hospital here on the coast—only a clinic, given that the new hospital hasn't opened up yet. If it's serious, we'll need to go to the hospital in the city," she replied softly, ignoring my statement completely.

"How will Opa get there?"

"They'll have to either fly him over by helicopter or by water taxi," Oma said. Then, she left my side to go to talk to one of the police officers.

The officer returned to me after talking with Rachelle. "I have questioned both the girl and her mom. They both say they were in their kitchen baking cookies. I'm not sure what you saw, but it wasn't her."

I was frustrated and angry, mostly at myself for not doing anything about the vision of the accident in the first place.

"Is it possible that the driver was trying to avoid a deer or some sort of animal? Also, his front right-side tire is blown, but we're not sure when that happened. We will do a complete investigation and let you know of the results. I'll ask Officer Riley to take you to the hospital."

The officer looked at me. His eyes were dark and angry.

18

REMAINS THE SAME—JULY 6TH, 4:30 PM

The policeman's eyes were just like Rachelle's had been yesterday. He began to grin at me, his mouth splitting across his face.

As we were getting into the police car, I asked Oma, "Oma, did you see that police officer's eyes?"

"No, why?"

"They were weird."

"What do you mean by weird, Orabella?"

"They looked dark or angry, but he was smiling." Even the thought of him gave me shivers.

"Orabella, when traumatic things happen, we become upset, and we start to see things that aren't there."

"Oma, I know what I saw. I could see Rachelle on the road."

An officer climbed into the front seat behind the wheel and turned to look at us. "The paramedics haven't been successful in treating him. They'll be driving him to the clinic. I'll drive you there."

“This can’t be happening,” Oma whispered as tears streamed down her cheeks.

After what seemed like an eternity, we finally arrived at the clinic. The ambulance was already there and was taking Opa in on the stretcher.

We both ran in but didn’t see any signs of Opa anywhere. A nurse at the front desk was ready for us. “Are you, Mrs. Van Dern Berg?”

“Yes, I am. How is my husband?”

“Your husband is with Dr. Thompson. The doctor will be out as soon as he can. Please, have a seat and let me know if you need anything while you wait.”

“Thank you,” Oma replied between sobs.

While we waited for the doctor to come, neither Oma nor I spoke. We only held each other tightly. After a while, a man came out of the double doors and approached us.

“Hello, I’m Dr. Thompson. Are you Mrs. Van Dern Berg?”

“Yes, I am. This is my granddaughter, Orabella,” Oma replied as we both stood up.

“Mrs. Van Dern Berg, your husband appears to have suffered a major head injury. The paramedics tried to revive him in the ambulance and continued to do so on the way here. I’m sorry to say, but your husband did not survive the car accident. I am truly sorry. We will be transferring him to Lions Gate Hospital for the final examination and will notify you of the results. I will be back soon to let you know when you can see him.”

Oma and I looked at each other and fell into each other’s arms, wracked with sobs. I couldn’t believe Opa was gone. I felt it was my fault.

I suddenly realized, *What if I could go back in time and warn Opa of the upcoming accident? What if I could prevent this from happening? What if I could save his life?*

I turned to Oma and said, "I just thought of something. What if I use the amulet to go back in time to warn Opa of the accident?"

"Orabella, have you gone back in time yet?" Oma asked as she brushed away the tears from her cheeks.

"Yes, I went back to Paris with Opa. I'll ask Wadjet to help me."

"I don't know, Orabella. It might be too dangerous. I'm sorry, but there's too much to think about right now." Oma dismissed my questions with a shake of her head.

"Oma, I'm just going to go to the bathroom. Do you want me to get you anything from the gift shop next door?" I was determined to change what had just happened.

"Orabella, give me a moment to think," she said as she sat down.

I walked down the hallway, looking for the bathroom. When I found it, I walked inside, and immediately an eerie feeling came over me, as if I was being watched. It was the same feeling of being followed, like back at the house. The light flickered above me, and the room started to turn cold. As I looked into the bathroom mirror to wash my face with cold water, I saw red eyes looking back at me. I quickly turned around, but there was nothing there. I looked back at the mirror, and the lights suddenly went out. Scared, I called out, "Help! The lights have gone out! I can't see!"

I heard people outside the door, and I called out again, "Hello, I need help! The lights have gone out! Please, help!"

Suddenly, the lights came back on, and I felt a hand touch my right shoulder. I ran to the door.

"Orabella, wait," the voice said.

I turned around; it was Morrigan. She was floating in the corner of the single-person restroom. It would have been a funny exchange, meeting a god in a bathroom stall, had I not been so angry at her.

"Why didn't you warn Opa or me earlier? Stop scaring me like that! I hate those red eyes!" I yelled.

"I don't have red eyes, but I did warn you when I first came to meet you," Morrigan said.

"But you didn't warn us of the accident. Also, if you didn't have red eyes, then whose eyes were they?"

"I did sense another presence when I came into the room, but it left quickly."

"So, what about Opa? If you can't save him, then I will go back in time to warn him. Now, tell me, why didn't you say anything about the accident?"

"I came here to let you know that I have given your Opa a safe passage to the other side."

"Well, thanks, but no thanks. You play games, and I don't like it. I can't trust you. Please, go away!" I hollered. I ran out of the bathroom and back to Oma.

"Oma, are you okay?" I asked.

"Yes, Bella, I'm doing okay," Oma said softly.

"Do you need anything? Are you hungry?"

"No, Bella, but you must be. Why don't you take a taxi back home and make yourself something to eat and try to rest? It won't be long. I need to see Opa and finalize some paperwork with the doctor."

"Really? Are you sure it's okay to go back by myself?"

"Yes, Bella. You're a big girl, and I trust you won't burn down the house," she said as she leaned into me to hug me. "You were very strong today. I am so proud of you."

"Okay, Oma. I'll see you at home." I couldn't wait to put on the amulet and get myself back in time. Opa was not gone!

"Here's some money for you to catch a cab."

"Thank you, Oma," I said as I wiped some tears from her cheeks and turned to exit the clinic. As I walked towards the exit, I noticed the gift shop sold cell phone chargers. I ran in and bought it with the money Oma gave me and hoped I had enough money left over for the taxi. *Alright! Let's get home to charge my phone and go back in time.*

There was a cab waiting at the front of the clinic. It was raining by then, and the wind blew it sideways, soaking me completely. I jumped into the taxi.

"Can you take me to 2489 Lockyear, please?"

"Of course, little lady," the cab driver said. "Are you related to Jasper?"

"Yes, I'm his granddaughter."

"Is Jasper okay? I heard about the accident," he said, looking at me through the rearview mirror, his eyes dropping with concern.

"No, Opa didn't make it," I whispered as tears came to my eyes.

"I'm so sorry for your loss. Jasper would always fix my shoes. He was a very nice man."

"Yes, he was." The tears in my eyes now flowed down onto my cheeks.

"I'm sorry I upset you."

"It's okay. It's just been a horrible day. Excuse me, but this is all the money I have. Will this be enough to get home?" I asked as tears rained down.

"More than enough. Don't worry, the ride is on me. Let's get you home."

"Thank you." As the taxi drove away, I cried even harder, sinking into the back seat.

I was back at the house within minutes. I jumped out of the taxi and ran to the front door to grab my cell phone, but out of the corner of my eye, I noticed a shadow at the back of the workhouse. Instead of going through the front door, I snuck around the side of the house and inched my way towards Opa's workspace.

My eyes were fixed on the shadow rummaging through the back house. As I got closer, I could almost make out its shape, but a sudden flurry of crows erupted from the trees all around me. At the eruption of sound, the trespasser immediately stopped ransacking the house, ran out the door, and bolted for the creek. Jet black hair trailed behind the figure. It was Rachelle.

I chased after her. She ran along the stream, heading towards the tire swing. I was gaining on her when she abruptly stopped and whirled around to face me. She had her hands on her hips defiantly. Surprised by her confrontation, I stopped dead in my tracks—only a few feet away from her. She raised her arm and wagged her finger at me to egg me on. The anger inside of me rose to a boil, and I closed the distance between us to come face to face with her.

"Orabella, you're breaking the law. You're on our property. Shall I call the police?"

"Rachelle, you are on *our* land. *You* are the one trespassing! Why are you sneaking around? And what were you doing up on the road when Opa's truck flipped?"

"What are you talking about? I was with Mom all day baking. I came outside to play down here. You're seeing things," Rachelle said snootily.

I took a deep breath but didn't respond. I turned around and ran back to the house.

"Hey! Where are you going?" Rachelle yelled after me.

I ignored her and just kept running. When I got into the house, I noticed right away how empty it felt. I ran upstairs to my bedroom, where Lolo was sleeping on my bed. She started meowing when I came into the room.

"Not now, Lolo. Opa is gone, and I need to go back in time to save his life. But first, I need to plug in my phone and charge it," I said, looking around for a power outlet.

"Ah-ha!" I found one and plugged it in. I sat down on the bed to pet Lolo and asked myself, *What was Rachelle doing in Opa's workspace?* I needed to get into the Shoe Chamber without her seeing me.

I jumped up from the bed and ran down the stairs and headed to the back door of the house, where I could surreptitiously run into the workhouse undetected—hopefully.

I ran to the workshop without seeing Rachelle, but being in Opa's space without him there felt so odd. I pushed aside a pang of sadness, ran to the back of his shed, and down the stairs to the Shoe Chamber with determination. I grabbed the amulet and held it to my chest.

"Okay, amulet. Take me back to earlier this morning so I can warn my Opa," I said softly.

There was nothing—no buzzing, no energy. It was like it was dead.

"Oh no, did I break it?" I tapped it against my chest but didn't feel anything. I put it down on the Book and commanded in a louder voice, "Amulet, take me back to this morning so I can warn my Opa!" Nothing happened. *Why isn't it working?*

"Is this a joke, Wadjet? Where are you?"

The room started to shake. *Are we having an earthquake?* I clung onto the chair to steady myself. As the room continued to quake, the dirt fell from the exposed roots of the ceiling, and shoes started falling out of their compartments from the walls. I shrieked in fear. What if I got trapped down here beneath so many layers of the earth?

Suddenly, a golden light blinded me. I kept my eyes closed until the light faded, and when it did, a huge golden falcon stood in front of me.

19

GOLDEN FALCON—JULY 6TH, 4:45 PM

The enormous falcon opened its sharp beak, its voice rumbling through the air like thunder. "You cannot interfere with what is meant to happen."

"What do you mean? Opa was meant to die?" I screamed at him.

"Yes, you are all going to die. You do not have a choice as to when or how. Orabella, you cannot go back in time and save him," Horus said.

"How did you know?" I asked, my mouth agape. "And why not? I have all these powers, why can't I use it to save him?"

Horus did not bother to answer how he knew my intentions. Instead, he said sternly, "You have these things specifically for your missions; you cannot use them outside of that. You would be serving *your* purpose and not the greater purpose."

"Listen, I totally get that, but why can't I just change this one thing?"

"Because then you would be changing reality according to your needs, and that is very much like what Iblis is doing. It is all self-serving. You can go back in time and prevent your Opa's accident, but there will be consequences for such actions that will be far worse than losing him. Either way, you end up coming back to this very moment, asking this same question."

I stopped and reflected on what I had been asking for. I was angry and frustrated, but I understood.

"If we all had these abilities to go back and change history according to what we wanted, there would be chaos," Horus said calmly.

"How is this different from the missions I'm supposed to go on? Aren't I changing history?"

"No, you are preventing history from being changed. Iblis lives outside the reality of man. The dimension he resides in is not affected by the consequences of his actions. But there is a cost that affects us all eventually if he succeeds. You are preventing pivotal moments in history from being changed, moments that inspired change and helped to inspire many more. It is this inspiration that helps the light grow and brings humanity closer together. Accept this moment and understand there are greater moments, and opportunities, ahead of you."

"I just want my Opa back!"

"Orabella, you are being driven by sheer emotion. Grow from this or allow the pain to devour you. It is your choice."

"It is not my choice that Opa is gone and left me to do this all alone," I whispered, my heart breaking all over again.

"You cannot be selfish and do something bigger than yourself. It will affect the timeline. Iblis works by dividing us. Instead, trust your gut. Do not be distracted by your notions of what you think happened. Iblis can mislead you into believing things to throw you off."

"What are you saying? Did Iblis cause the accident?"

"Iblis created a situation to avert your focus," Horus said with finality.

"This is not a game. My Opa is dead. He is gone," I said and started crying again.

"Yes, he is. He was a great Soljourner and served us well."

"So why would you not protect him from Iblis then?" I said as tears ran down my cheeks.

"Orabella, Jasper was a well-trained Soljourner who completed all of his missions and was preparing to teach the last Soljourner. He had the power to protect himself."

"You didn't answer my question. Why would you not have saved Opa?"

"You must understand that there are things that are supposed to happen for a reason."

"First you tell me it was an accident, and then you tell me that it was meant to happen. I don't understand."

"You need to grieve the loss of your mentor. You need to let go before you can move forward. Remember what Wadjet is teaching you about controlling your thoughts and feelings. The amulet will not work if you direct it from your emotions."

And with that, the falcon was gone.

"Wait, come back! You never answered my question. Couldn't you have saved Opa? I hate you—I hate all of you!" I shouted, pounding my fists into my legs.

Then it hit me: Opa was gone forever. I felt a pain I had never felt before. Opa was gone. My dad and mom were gone. The falcon was gone. *I am all alone.*

I felt a pain in my chest. As I breathed, the pain became more and more unbearable. It was the feeling of overwhelming sadness. I felt the darkness caving in on me. Lolo brushed up against me, but I was in too much pain to want her comfort, so I pushed her away. "Go away, Lolo. Leave me alone."

I ran up the stairs to the workshop bathroom, slammed the door, and was left in complete darkness. I fell to the floor, crying under the weight of my grief. I could see Lolo's paw reaching under the bathroom door, but all I wanted was to be alone.

I looked in the mirror and saw the pain. My heart ached. I had grown so close to him. He taught me so much. What would I become without him? First, my dad and mom, and now Opa. I was afraid of loving or caring for anyone else if all they did was leave.

I hated Rachelle. I knew it was her fault. She was such a horrible person who just wanted to ruin my life. What had I done to her to deserve this?

The tears burned down my cheeks, and my chest grew tighter with each breath. I could no longer feel my legs or feet, almost as if I was frozen. What was the point of all of this? If I was this special Soljourner, then why were things so hard? Why was Opa taken from us?

I curled up in the corner of the bathroom, the darkness closing in around me, my thoughts growing heavier with each passing breath that separated me from life. I was alone and felt, for the first time, that division that Oma had talked about: the black wolf and the white wolf.

I was curled up on the bathroom floor because I wanted to go back to where it felt safe—back to the place where there was no pain or loss. Everything was so clouded and confusing right now. I thought I broke free of Rachelle's hold over me, but I was powerless once again.

I felt myself slipping, not unlike a dream in which I would fall. I fell somewhere within myself that was dark—a place that held all those things that fed the black wolf. I could feel the coldness, yet the pain was hot and burned through me. *A cold fire? How is that possible?* I stood up, feeling dizzy. The room seemed distorted. I reached out and clung to the sink. I grabbed hold of it with both hands to pull myself up and look in the mirror.

I was shocked and scared at what was looking back. Red eyes were staring back at me. The bathroom turned cold, and the darkness surrounded me like nothing I had ever experienced. It felt dirty, like I needed a shower to scrub myself. What I saw wasn't me, but it was. I saw the red eyes behind me in the mirror. I knew he had come for me.

It was Iblis. "Did you not get any answers to your questions, little one? You will be left to wonder why, and you will be filled with the guilt of all that you should have done, could have done . . . You have so much power, yet you couldn't save your Opa. You poor little girl; you have no power at all. You are naive to think that you could make an ounce of difference when it was too easy to get rid of your mother, father, and grandfather."

"Stop!" I screamed at the top of my lungs. I wished I had the amulet with me, as I felt the darkness closing in on me. There was no hope left in me to fight. My breath was shallow, and I could barely get any air. I sunk to the floor, hyperventilating. Finally, I realized I needed to change my mindset. I needed to breathe. I centred my focus on only that. The feeling of falling stopped and I began to float above it. I broke free.

Suddenly the bathroom became quiet. The raucous voice of Iblis was silent, and the force around me slowly dissipated. The room became lighter, and I could finally take a deep, cleansing breath. I felt both energized and exhausted. I knew this was not the end of the battle of wills with Iblis. It was only the beginning. Awareness, focus, and practice of being still from all the distractions would keep me grounded. It was time for me to rest and be prepared for what tomorrow would bring. But for one small moment tonight, the light won from my power of choice, and with each decision towards the light, I would become more powerful.

I walked out of the bathroom, and Lolo danced around my ankles. Too weak to pet her, I rushed to the workshop door. The room was spinning and my stomach hurt. I felt too weak to open it, but with all of my strength, I began to push through the entrance, and the rush of fresh air helped me. I felt dizzy, and the cramps in my lower belly were so painful. I bent over to ease the pain. Oma had just arrived at the house in the taxi, and she jumped out and ran to me.

"Orabella, are you okay?" she asked.

"Oma, I'm having pain in my lower belly."

"Okay, let's get you into the house and into the shower. You're sweating a lot."

We stumbled into the house and went up to the bathroom. I undressed and got into the shower, and the hot water fell on me with coursing relief. I began to feel lighter and cleaner. I had won another challenge. Rachelle yesterday, Iblis today.

I got out of the shower, dried off, put on my pyjamas, and walked out in the hallway. Oma was standing there with big tears in her eyes, which made me cry, and we hugged each other.

"Oma, I want to sleep in my bed tonight."

"Really? Are you sure?"

"Yes, so I know you're close by."

"Of course. Get your rest. I'll see you in the morning." Oma followed me to my room. The lights were already on, and Lolo was lying at the head of my bed.

"Goodnight, Bella. I love you." She gave me a big hug.

"I love you too, Oma," I said with a smile as I squeezed her back. Turning around before leaving, I asked, "Oma, what do I do now with my training?"

"Well, from my end, we will start your homeschooling and prepare you for your first mission. I'm going to leave the door open tonight, so if you need anything, I'm just a holler away. I don't think I'm going to get much sleep tonight."

"Did you hear back from the hospital as to what happened to Opa?"

"Not yet. Probably in a few days, the coroner's office will be calling." Tears were heavy in Oma's eyes. I didn't want to ask her any more questions to upset her.

"Good night, Bella."

"Good night, Oma."

Oma walked out and headed to her bedroom, where she kept her door open. I pulled back the sheets and lay in bed with the lights on. Lolo was on top of my chest, purring. I stroked her head and began to cry again as I thought about Opa and the day we went fishing.

I reached up and turned out the lights, and Lolo slid down next to me. I lay there in the dark, feeling uneasy, like something was about to happen. I started thinking about the shadow in my dream but tried to push the thought away. My eyelids grew heavy, and I began to fall into my vision, back to the tree with the falcon flying overhead. It was so beautiful there. What appeared to be translucent water was around the tree, and it held an endless view of the universe in all directions. I could see a figure in the tree and I walked towards it. I soon realized I was not in a dream but back at the centre of the universe.

The figure in the tree became more prominent and materialized as a human walking out of the trunk. It was my friend, Ara, and for a moment I was so excited to see a familiar face, but then her eyes flashed green and my face fell because I remembered it was Wadjet.

"Hello, Orabella. You have had many challenges in the last few days, and I see our training can advance with success, as you have not let your emotions lead you to make poor decisions."

"Yes, it is hard, but I understand fully now what I need to do during times when I am not in control of my environment. I know now how to let go."

"Very good, Orabella. Now that you have learned to breathe through your emotions and to observe them without reacting, we can focus on making you physically stronger and quicker. You must be strong emotionally, mentally, physically, and spiritually on your own, and then you will have the full power of the amulet."

"So, what's next?" I asked.

"I feel that you are very close to the physical transformation into womanhood."

"Is that related to my special gift?"

"No, what I am referring to is that you are close to your cycle of life: the power to give birth."

"Oh, are you talking about my Moon Time?"

"Yes, an extraordinary time, since you will soon be in full connection with the feminine life force through the Tree of Life. With this transformation into womanhood, you will be able to become even more powerful."

"Well, it doesn't feel that way."

"Orabella, as you become more in tune with the rhythms of the body and the universal feminine energy, those physical challenges will go away. You will be in the flow of the Tree of Life and all of its energy through the amulet."

"Well, that's good to know. Not feeling so hot about all this transformation stuff," I said, remembering the horrible cramps and lightheadedness.

"Georgia, or Didu Mu, will be coming back to see you soon to start your homeschooling with your Oma. You may have to go to China and spend time in Mt. Hengshan at the Hanging Temple, which is over one thousand years old."

"That sounds cool, but Opa said when I did my training at the Shoe Chamber, time would be slower there. Why can't Georgia train me there instead of China?"

"Excellent question. The goddesses have difficulty staying in their forms here on the Earth plane. They need to go to the Vortex that brings them into this world. It is where they are closest to their dimension. The further they travel from the Vortex, the harder it is for them to stay in this dimension."

"Oh, I get it now."

"Now, I want you to focus on three things. First, I want you to picture Rachelle and tell me when you feel something."

"Okay, I feel some anger but not a lot."

"Good. Now I want you to picture Iblis."

"Okay, I feel fear but more anger now."

"Good. I want you to visualize Opa's accident. What do you feel?"

"I feel sad, but more than that, the I have feelings of anger and fear."

"Good. I want you to visualize Iblis and Rachelle looking at your Opa as he is dying."

I felt my anger shoot right up, hard to control, but I also felt the sadness and the fear. I felt like it was turning into a tornado. I started to feel like I was losing control of it. I remembered the tornado from the *Wizard of Oz*, and what Opa said about Dorothy's journey.

My emotions kept switching from fear to anger to sadness, all whirling around me in a storm of uncontrollable energy. I focused on my breathing and tried to go to that place of floating. Instead, an actual tornado appeared in front of me, pulling everything around me into it, including the Tree. I couldn't see Wadjet. I started to panic.

Then, I remembered what Opa said: "Orabella, you can't make this journey alone. Friends are here to help you."

"Wadjet, I need your help!" I screamed out over the howling winds.

Wadjet appeared in front of me and grabbed my hand. I slowed down my breathing. I breathed in the feelings, and the tornado got smaller and smaller until it disappeared.

"Very good, Orabella. Your Opa and Oma have taught you well. Yes, no matter how powerful or confident you think you are, there are times you will need friends, so do not ever hesitate to ask for help on your missions, or anytime in life."

"Thank you, Wadjet. Thank you so much." I wanted to reach out and hug her.

The form of Ara changed and I saw Wadjet as her true self.

"I forgot to tell you the last time, but you are so beautiful Wadjet."

"Thank you, Orabella. I am happy to hear my form pleases you. I cannot do it for very long in your dimension, but I am so proud of what you have accomplished with your training."

20

SAYING GOODBYE—JULY 8TH, 3:24 PM

I had about two days of rest after my training with Wadjet. I doodled designs for my superhero costume, and I texted my friends. I had to answer quite a few texts since it had been over a week since I left home. I didn't tell anyone what had happened to my mom and dad. I only said that there was a family emergency and I had to leave right away. That was why I was staying with my grandparents. Scarlett was texting me puns every hour. Olivia was still in Europe. I also caught up with Alexa, Jacquie, Georgia, Camille, Ava, Ara, Quincy, Trinity, Remi, and the rest of the Girl Squad.

My thumb was sore from texting back so many of them, finding out which high school everybody was going to and what their summer plans were. And, of course, they were all asking what my birthday plans were, which I didn't want to think about, as today was Opa's funeral.

I had never felt so much sadness in my life. I had never been to a funeral before, and from what Auntie Adri told me, she wasn't giving a traditional send-off. She was trying to do something special for Opa that would be a surprise for Oma.

With Opa gone, who was going to help guide me? Wadjet? Oma? How would Oma help me with my training? I had already lost my mom and dad, but this felt much more permanent, more real. Mom and Dad's disappearance still felt like a dream. These thoughts ran through my head as I sat on my bed in my room. The feelings were so overwhelming that I was afraid to move, knowing that things would change once again. I wanted to help but didn't know how.

I finally got off of my bed and put on a black dress that Oma got for me in town. My cheeks and eyes were red from crying; my heart was heavy.

I slowly went downstairs and crept into the kitchen. Oma was standing at the kitchen sink, also wearing a black dress. She was still, but as I was about to speak, she turned and looked at me. She said, "Oh, right. I was about to come to get you. We're going to leave in a bit. You look very grown up in that dress, Orabella."

"Thank you, Oma. You look very beautiful today," I said with a sad smile.

"Well, we should get going. Auntie Adri says she will meet us there. I'm not sure what she's up to."

We didn't say much to each other as we walked to the truck that Oma had borrowed from a friend. It was the first time that I would see Oma drive. *She knows how to drive, right?* I thought to myself nervously. She started the engine and slowly drove off the farm and onto the road towards the secret cove where we were having the funeral. We were both quiet. Oma seemed a little nervous driving, so I turned on the radio to ease the tension. The song that came on was "Somewhere Over the Rainbow," and we started to laugh and cry at the same time. I looked out the passenger side window and saw that the sun was trying, almost struggling, to burst through the layer of clouds.

I didn't know what to say to Oma. All I knew was that I missed Opa. As we began to get closer to the cove, we noticed a long lineup of cars and the beginnings of a large crowd. Oma's eyes widened. I couldn't believe it myself. I never expected to see so many people. People waved our truck to the front, where a spot was reserved for us. As we got out of the car, Auntie Adri came over to us.

"Audrey, I hope this isn't too much," Auntie said.

"Adri, I'm speechless. Thank you."

Person after person came up to Oma to hug her. I held on tightly to Oma's hand as we walked the trail from the road down to the water. There were a few people I recognized from town, but none stood out enough for me to comfortably go up to them and talk to them. Since Opa didn't have much of an extended family, it was only me, Oma, and Auntie. I wished Mom and Dad were there.

The sun was slowly setting, and a burst of yellow and orange light broke through the clouds. The crowd became silent. Oma, Auntie, and I slowly walked towards a gazebo with a microphone. We entered the structure and sat down in, and after a few minutes, Oma stood up and spoke.

"To those I love and those who love me,

When I am gone, release me and let me go.

I have so many things to see and do.

You must not tie yourself to me with tears,

Be happy that we have had so many years.

I gave you my love—you can only guess
How much you gave me happiness.
I thank you for the love each has shown,
But I know it's time I travel alone.
So, grieve a while for me if you must.
Then let your grief be comforted by trust.
It's only for a while that we must part,
So bless the memories with your heart.
I won't be far away, for life goes on.
Though you can't see or touch me, I'll be near.
And if you listen with your heart,
You will have all my love around you soft and dear,
And when you must come this way alone,
I'll greet you with a smile and say,
'Welcome Home'!

"These are the words of a man who cared so much about the world," Oma said. "He was an amazing husband, father, and grandfather. Jasper was a beacon of light for his family and community. He was our hero. To even have this sort of gathering now would have made him very uncomfortable.

"Jasper was very humble and unassuming. Not a man of many words, but he was a man of many deeds. He showed his kindness and was always there to support others. Jasper will still be with us always. Thank you for attending. It means the world to our family and me. Never take your life and time with family and friends for granted; life can change in a moment."

There were only the sounds of the waves and soft cries that blended. Then, Auntie, Oma, and I went to the shore, and everyone else followed. Oma and Auntie put the ashes from the urn into a small paper boat and lit a candle. I looked out at the ocean and noticed a raven and a falcon flying overhead. *Hmm, is that Morrigan and Horus?*

We put the boat in the water and pushed it off. The boat got about halfway to the cove before it was lit ablaze, and the crowd behind us started to sing "Into the Mystic" by Van Morrison, one of Opa's favourite songs. Off in the distance, a foghorn sounded.

I felt my heartache. I tried not to cry, but I couldn't hold it in anymore. I stood up and held Oma tight, not only for my sorrow, but for hers. The flame and the paper boat slowly disappeared, engulfed by the water. As we walked back to the truck together, the song "Flashlight" by Jessie J. started to play over the loudspeaker, and everybody began to pull out their flashlights and swing them in the air in time to the music. It was like a gift from the town.

"What is this?" Oma said. She started to cry and laugh at the same time.

"Audrey, this was Orabella's idea, so I went into town and handed out flyers to tell everybody to learn the song and bring their flashlights," Auntie Adri said.

"Oh my. Opa would have loved that," Oma replied softly. "Thank you both. This means the world to us . . . to me."

Oma gave us a big hug, and I began to mouth the words to the song. I cried even more. Opa was our flashlight. Every few steps, somebody stopped us to hug Oma and to tell her stories of what Opa did for them in their life. Some stories surprised Oma because they were things Opa never mentioned—little things, like pulling over and helping somebody change a tire, or helping a cat out of a tree or a dog out of a ditch, or offering to fix shoes for free. After all, they were low on money. They were deeds of kindness that were never mentioned afterward. It was a story accumulated over time by the community about how much Jasper was valued as an everyday hero.

By the time we got to Oma's friend's truck, it was entirely dark. The parade of cars soon began to fill the road behind us.

"Audrey, I have to go. I need to catch the last ferry back to Vancouver," Auntie Adri told her.

"You're not staying?"

"I can't, I have to work in the morning, but I'll be back soon. I'm sorry I'm missing your birthday tomorrow."

"Okay. I'll miss you tomorrow, Auntie."

We all hugged, and Auntie headed off to her car. We got into the truck, and the ride home was quiet. A song was playing on the radio, and Oma slowly reached for the knob to turn it off but hesitated and returned her hand to the wheel. As we approached the spot where Opa died, Oma slowed down for a moment, and time felt like it stood still. I had goosebumps on my arms and neck. We pulled into the driveway. Oma put the truck in park but took a while to turn it off. Her eyes were closed and tears rolled down her cheeks. Oma had been so strong throughout the day, and now it was her time to let go. I reached out to hold her hand, and when she turned to me to hug me, she finally let go. She cried for a few minutes.

Gathering herself, she said, "Thank you, Bella. I appreciate all the support you've given me. I couldn't have been so strong today without you. How are you doing?"

"I'm good, Oma. We made it through together."

"Yes, indeed, Bella. We have. Are you hungry?"

"No, Oma. I just want to go to bed," I replied tiredly.

"Me too, but there is one last thing we need to do."

"Okay. What is it, Oma?"

"Well, we need to spread the rest of Opa's ashes around the base of the tree out back," Oma replied.

"We have more ashes?"

"Yes, the boat would have sunk if I used them all. Besides, this is what Opa wanted so he would be close to us."

We headed to the tree where Oma pulled out the urn and opened it. We were about to spread Opa's ashes around the base of the tree when a gust of cold wind came up and Morrigan appeared.

"Hello, I hope I did not scare you this time," Morrigan said.

"Who are you?" Oma said, putting the lid back on the urn and holding it close to her.

"Oma, this is Morrigan."

"Why are you here?" Oma asked in an annoyed, tired voice.

"I wanted to give my last respects to Jasper and give him safe passage to the other side."

"You what?" Oma yelled.

I intervened to try to calm Oma down. "Oma, Morrigan is the goddess of death and provides souls who have died safe passage to the afterlife."

"I know who you are. Jasper warned me not to trust you," Oma said with uncharacteristic harshness.

There was an awkward silence before Oma sighed and spoke again in her usual gentle voice. “Well then, thank you.”

Morrigan suddenly changed into a raven and flew off. Oma and I were left there crying. I didn’t expect such kind words like that from Morrigan.

“She’s an interesting character, Orabella,” Oma said.

“She looks so beautiful but scary,” I said in return.

“Yes, I agree.”

Oma’s hand was shaking as she slowly removed the lid from the urn. She bent down and poured Opa’s ashes onto the base of the tree. We were quiet for a moment, and Oma seemed deep in thought.

“Okay, Bella, it’s been a long day. Let’s head off to bed.”

“Looking forward to it,” I said, grateful the day was over.

We got back to the house, and a quiet, eerie feeling had come over it. We went our separate ways and got ready for bed. As I brushed my teeth, I thought about Oma. I couldn’t imagine what she was going through. To lose somebody that had been a constant for her whole life, a life spectacularly different than she could have ever imagined. The pain she must have felt. I didn’t know what to do or say—only to hug her. I got into bed.

As I drifted off, I remembered it was my birthday tomorrow. I didn’t feel like celebrating, and I didn’t want to remind Oma about it. A wave of heaviness and sadness fell over me as I fell asleep. I began to dream that it was my birthday, and I was blowing out my candles. Everybody was there: Oma and Opa, Mom and Dad. We were all happy and we were all together. Suddenly, everybody got up and walked out of the room, and I was alone except for somebody standing in the corner, hiding in the shadows. Was it Iblis or Morrigan?

The dark shadow blinked open its red eyes and said, "There is a spy very close to you who is serving the light and the dark."

"What? Who?" I said, feeling my heart pound against my chest.

"You are closer to finding out who it is," the shadow said.

21

BIRTH DAY—JULY 9TH, 7:30 AM

When I woke up, the sun was shining brightly outside. I rubbed the sleep from my eyes and remembered it was my birthday. Usually, I would have jumped out of bed in excitement for this day, but this year was so different. My heart was heavy. A lot had happened in just over a week. I lay in bed a little while longer. My body was tired from the funeral yesterday. Downstairs, I could hear Oma making breakfast. I slowly got out of bed and got dressed in my favourite cat shirt, groggily shuffling towards the kitchen. Oma was sitting at the table, reading. When she heard me come in, she lowered her book and looked at me with a warm but tired smile.

"Good morning, Bella. How did you sleep?"

"I slept okay. How did you sleep, Oma?" I did not want to tell Oma about the dream with the message about the spy.

"I slept okay. I was just thinking about all the chores to do today."

I just stood there, not sure what to say, when Oma stood up and hugged me.

"Happy Birthday, sweetie!"

"Thanks, Oma." I gave her an extra big hug.

"Okay, birthday girl, before you squeeze the poop out of me, your present is in the living room."

"Really? OH MY GOD! Thank you, Oma."

I turned around and ran to the living room, nearly tripping over myself in my excitement. There was a large box wrapped in silver paper sitting on the couch. I started ripping it open, and tissue paper flew everywhere. It was a book of quotes by Helen Keller, who I loved. Even though she lost her sight and her hearing, she never stopped helping others. She inspired me to be strong, no matter what obstacles presented themselves. Beneath the book was clothing, but as I ran my fingers over the fabric, it was evident that this wasn't just any ordinary clothing. I looked up from my present as Oma came into the room.

"Thank you, Oma. I love Helen Keller. My mom would read quotes to me from her book all the time," I said, smiling at her.

"I know. I used to do the same with your mom."

"Really? Mom never told me that! That's so cool! I noticed another gift under the book."

"This is from Opa and me. We worked on it together. We felt a heroine needed a proper outfit."

I pulled it out entirely from the box and held it in front of my face. It was a smooth, shiny fabric in bright colours. The top was a long, magenta tunic with gold trim, and the pants were a gorgeous aquamarine colour.

"Wow, my superhero costume! I love it!" As I looked closer, there were small rivets in the stitching.

"Oma, what are these for?" I asked, feeling each little bump in the fabric, like tiny beads had been sewn into it.

"I sewed crystals into the lining of the fabric for protection. I hope you don't mind that I designed this from your sketches I saw on the desk in the Shoe Chamber."

"Wow. Thank you, Oma."

"Keep looking. There's more in the box," Oma said.

I looked again and found a pair of emerald-coloured shoes.

"OH MY GOD, I love them!"

"Jasper made them for you. He was so impressed with himself that he decided these would be the last shoes he would ever make."

"Really, Oma?" I loved the shoes, but I felt heavy with sadness. I missed Opa. I hugged the shoes tightly to my chest.

"I'm so glad you like everything," Oma said.

I looked at the clothes in amazement. Then, I looked up and asked a question that had just occurred to me, "Oma, how far back in time can I go?"

"You can only go back as far as the creation of the first Soljourner—back to Ancient Egypt. But keep in mind, the further back in time you go, the more exhausting the journey and the more displaced time is."

"What does it mean if time is displaced?" I asked curiously, still running the fabric through my fingertips.

"It means that time becomes more stretched out. The layering between dimensions is thinner, so there is a risk of slipping into another dimension."

I grew silent. That sounded dangerous.

Oma chuckled softly to brush away my fear of getting trapped in time. She grabbed some of the wrapping paper off the floor and said, "Don't worry about that right now, Bella. With the experience you gain from each mission, you will soon be able to handle anything that comes your way. And of course, you aren't alone. I will help you."

"But what about you, Oma? How can I help you? What will you do without the income from the shoe business?"

"Hush! You don't need to worry about that!" My Oma smiled at me with her kind eyes. "We have a trust fund that we can draw from that's been passed down from Soljourner to Soljourner. There's even been a secret benefactor who has helped us financially along the way."

"Who is it?" I asked.

"I don't know. I have only heard stories. But enough about that. Do you want birthday cake for breakfast?"

"Oh, boy, do I!" My eyes lit up in excitement.

"It's your favourite: double chocolate!"

"Where did you get it?" I asked, a little bit of drool escaping the corner of my mouth.

"Auntie brought it over yesterday morning. She snuck it into the house without you seeing."

Oma went to the kitchen and came back with the cake. She lit three candles and started singing 'Happy Birthday.' *Wow, I can't believe I'm thirteen years old—officially a teenager.* I blew out the candles with Oma and then started to cry.

"I miss Opa," I whispered.

"I know. So do I," Oma said with tears falling down her cheeks.

"I'm sorry, Oma. I don't want to upset you."

"You haven't. If anything, I'm happy you thought of Opa when you were blowing out the candles."

I proceeded to cut the cake and pulled out six slices in total.

"Who are all these slices for?"

"Well, they're for you, me, Opa, Mom, Dad, and Auntie."

A few more tears fell down Oma's face in response.

We ended up sitting out on the porch, eating our pieces of cake. We were both quiet as we ate, but I finished mine rather quickly and jumped up.

"Oma, would you like to go for a walk?"

"No, Bella. Go without me. I have a few errands to run, and I need to clean up. But I think you need to wash the chocolate off your face first."

"I think I'll keep it there, just in case I want a snack." We both laughed.

"Do you need help with the dishes, Oma?"

"Oh, go enjoy your walk—it's okay."

As I walked out of the house, I thought of Dad, Mom, and Opa and how I missed them. Time was passing too quickly. It was slipping through my fingertips. The feeling of being out of control gave me that usual nervous feeling in my stomach. And seemingly from out of nowhere, Lolo came over and rubbed herself against my leg. I reached down, picked her up, and cuddled her against me.

Once again, her purring helped calm me down. What would I do without my little protector? I apologized to her for my previous outburst and kissed her on the top of her head. We sat down by the tree, and I started thinking about my friends at home.

My thoughts were interrupted when I heard Oma calling for me, and I rushed to the front of the house.

"Orabella, your cell phone is ringing nonstop," Oma said when she saw me coming.

I grabbed the phone out of Oma's hand and scrolled through my phone history. I had missed calls from everyone in the Girl Squad!

My phone buzzed. One text from Scarlett said:

Happy birthday. In heaven, all you get for your birthday is an angel food cake.

Wait, I have another pun for you.

Of course, you did, Scarlett.

If you spent your day in a well, can you say your day is well-spent?

Wow, that was bad. I laughed to myself.

I stood on the porch for over an hour, texting all the girls back, including Auntie to thank her for the birthday cake. I could see Oma grinning in the background, and my fingers finally got tired of texting.

"Was it nice connecting with your friends?" Oma asked.

"Yes, it was awesome. Oma, when can we go to Vancouver to see my friends? Maybe I can stay at Auntie's for a couple of days?"

"Well, let me think about it. There's a lot of chores to be done, and we have to get your homeschooling started, Orabella."

"Sounds good, Oma. Could I have some more birthday cake and go try on my costume?"

"Of course, it's your birthday, but don't eat too much. It'll keep you up tonight. Let me know if any adjustments need to be made to the costume."

I grabbed my superhero outfit, the Helen Keller book, and a couple of pieces of birthday cake, and headed to my room. I tried on the superhero clothes and checked myself out in the mirror. I looked awesome. I loved the shoes and gold trim. I swung around and did different poses.

I yelled out to Oma, "I love it, Oma! It fits perfectly!" I walked out onto the landing. Oma walked out of the kitchen and stood at the bottom of the stairs to look up at me.

"Well, it does indeed look perfect on you. Opa would be very proud." Our eyes started to fill with tears again, and we both smiled. I headed back to my room, and Oma headed back to the kitchen. I lay down on my bed and started reading the Hellen Keller book. Between chapters, I returned the texts I got from my friends.

After a restless night's sleep from too much chocolate birthday cake, I woke up early to go out to the workhouse. I grabbed a banana off the top of the fridge on my way out.

When I got into the Shoe Chamber, I immediately sat next to the Emerald Book and pried the amulet off of the cover. I wasn't sure how long I sat there for, grasping the amulet in my hand, when I heard the door open and footsteps hurried down the stairs. Oma entered the room somewhat flustered. With shallow breaths, she got out, "I've been looking everywhere for you."

I looked up at her. "Sorry, Oma."

"You have a special visitor at the house!"

"Who is it, Oma? Another one of those goddess girls?"

"It is, but something about her is different. The strength of her presence is undeniable."

My heart was pounding with a feeling of shared excitement.

"Oma, who is it?"

Oma was still breathless. "Orabella, the girl is Maat, and from my accounts of history, Maat is the daughter of the all-powerful being of Ra—of life itself."

"Wow, she sounds pretty cool," I said in awe from my chair.

"Come on! Let's not keep her waiting!" Oma said, her eyes sparkling brightly. I jumped up, put the amulet back on the cover of the Book, and followed her to the house. Oma was walking extra quickly to get back to our guest.

As we went through the front door, I could feel a lightness—a strange feeling—almost as if I were walking on a trampoline. The visitor was sitting at the kitchen table with her back to us, her long, blonde hair cascading over the back of the chair. When she heard us enter, she slowly stood up without turning, and I guessed we were about the same height. When she turned around, my mouth dropped open.

Maat looked exactly like my best friend Olivia. However, her appearance kept phasing in and out of looking like Olivia and looking like an Egyptian goddess. Her blonde hair would darken to black, Olivia's fair skin would become a sun-kissed copper, and her youthful stature would sprout to that of a tall and regal woman. Over and over the figure before me shifted and altered. But what was most arresting of all were her eyes. They were like looking through a telescope. Like all of the universes were contained within them.

Then, she spoke in a voice that was like the ringing of a bell. "It is a pleasure to meet you, Orabella. I have taken notice of your journey to become a Soljourner. However, many things have become unbalanced. I am here to set the balance back in order, but I need your help to do so. We must prepare immediately." Her voice never fully stopped making the sound. It carried through the air with a resonating hum.

"Wh-What do we need to do?" I stammered.

"Orabella, it is about Horus, the creator of your kind. He has taken something and has disturbed the balance of time, creating havoc for all of us, including me," Maat said, her voice beautiful and lonely at the same time.

"How is that possible? You're so powerful," I said, lowering my head in reverence.

"I cannot say at this point, Orabella. What is more disturbing is that it appears your father, Marcus, helped him steal it."

"What? Dad? Is he still alive?" My head snapped back up and I looked Maat directly in her eyes. "Why would he help Horus steal something?"

Maat did not flinch or change at all at my abruptness. "It appears your father assisted Horus in stealing a powerful weapon that has thrown off the balance of light and dark, and yes, your father is still alive."

Both Oma and I let out a sigh of relief, knowing that Dad was alive.

"Where is he now? Where is my mom?" I asked as tears ran down my cheeks. I felt so conflicted. I was happy that my dad was alive but horrified that he had done something terrible. Was he the spy that I was warned about in my dream?

"Orabella, I cannot sense where your mother is, but she is neither alive nor dead, and I cannot find your father either. It seems Horus has cloaked him—or perhaps even both of your parents. Has Horus contacted you all?"

"Yes, just after Opa died, he appeared to me," I said, and then I came to a horrible conclusion. "Is Horus working with Iblis?"

Maat's eyes glittered brightly before she answered. "No, what Horus has planned is something far more significant and more hideous than what Iblis has planned. Orabella, can you please retrieve the amulet for me? We must work together on this."

I turned and walked out of the kitchen to get the amulet from the workhouse and Oma followed. When we were out of earshot, I said, "Oma, wow, she's pretty cool. Her eyes are incredible!"

"Yes, it's hard not to stare at them."

"Do you trust her, Oma?"

"It's hard to say, Orabella, but she knows where your mom and dad are."

I opened the door to the workspace, and we picked our way through Opa's crowded workshop. It made me smile to see that one thing hadn't changed. We reached the back door, but before opening it, I asked Oma, "What if she's tricking us? Why did she ask me to go get the amulet? Considering how powerful she is, why couldn't she meet us in the Shoe Chamber like how Wadjet and Morrigan have?"

Oma grabbed the handle of the door. "Good point, but then again, she seemed to be having a tough time keeping her form, so maybe she's weaker in this dimension."

As Oma finished her sentence, she swung open the door and we started our descent down the spiral staircase. As we neared the last step, the wooden door to the Shoe Chamber crashed open, and a green flash almost blinded us. The loud vibration coming from the room was deafening. The light was coming from the Book and the amulet.

"Wow, it's so bright and noisy, Oma."

"Noisy? What do you mean, Orabella? I don't hear anything."

"You don't hear that loud buzz?"

"No, but the bright green light is giving me a headache."

We entered the Shoe Chamber. The buzzing was so loud I had to clap my hands over my ears. Oma stood by the door, shielding her eyes from the light, while I walked over to the Book to pick up the amulet. As I drew closer, I realized it was the book itself that was glowing and vibrating. The vibrations were giving off the loud humming sound. Even after I took the amulet off of the Book, the noise continued. I stored the amulet in my pocket, and I could feel it buzzing against my leg.

Oma and I walked back to the house, and—through the window—I could see Maat talking to Lolo. Lolo was on the table, eye-level to Maat. As we entered the house, I could hear that Maat was speaking a different language to Lolo. I walked back into the kitchen and they both looked at me, a bright green flash running through their eyes.

"I noticed that you were talking with Lolo. Can you talk to animals too?"

"I can with *special kinds* of animals," Maat replied, smiling.

"Why is she special?"

"Nobody told you why Lolo is here for you?"

"It's been mentioned a few times."

"When you were born, your parents and grandparents asked Horus to help protect you. Horus called upon Bast, the Egyptian Cat Goddess, who gifted you a Guardian Cat. Lolo is Bast's strongest soldier—she's a warrior. Lolo is your dream protector."

"I knew she was special, but wow, thank you for giving me more insight," I said as I stroked Lolo's back. She began to purr.

"We also received the assistance of Breksta, the goddess of the night, a ruler over dreams, dreamers, and prophecies. Breksta keeps watching over your dreams from sunset to sunrise. She sealed the gates of your dreams and unconscious thoughts to any intruders."

"Wow, so are you saying my dreams would have been scarier?"

"Indeed. Your dreams are a gateway between time and dimensions; they can allow you to travel anywhere in all of existence. Soljourners receive messages within dreams, as it is much easier for gods to communicate with humans in Dreamtime."

"Is that true, Oma? About Lolo?"

Oma kept her distance and stood by the doorway between the kitchen and dining room. She answered from where she was standing. "Yes, that is correct, Orabella. We wanted to ensure your safety. We also made sure to never ask you about your dreams since we didn't want you to question them. We felt that by not saying anything, they would become routine for you.

"I am sorry that we didn't say anything to you earlier about your dreams, but as a family, we tried to shield you from what would eventually happen."

"Maat, why did you appear here in the kitchen and not in the Shoe Chamber as Wadjet and Morrigan did?"

"Quite simply, I cannot be underground. I need open space to be able to travel between dimensions," she answered.

Before I could ask any more questions, Maat stood up.

"Thank you for bringing the amulet to me, Orabella."

22

GIFT REVEALED—JULY 10TH, 9:05 AM

I took the amulet out of my pocket. The buzzing was quieter but still audible, and the glow was piercing. It cast a green light that danced across the entire kitchen.

Maat took the amulet from me and grabbed my hand. The room started to spin. I closed my eyes to stop the revolutions, but then, I felt my stomach flip-flop. I opened my eyes to see that I had been taken back to the centre of the universe. The kitchen was gone, Oma nowhere to be seen. Only Maat remained, standing next to me. Her face was still that of my friend, Olivia, but her hair was jet black and the clothing she wore looked to be made of pure gold.

I caught figures of all different forms and colours moving out of the shadows around the Tree of Life. Then, some slight stirring in the corner of my eye caught my attention and I realized that Lolo was standing right next to me. However, she was no longer my cuddly pet, but a woman about ten feet tall. She had the head of a golden cat, but her body was human. She stood at attention like a guard.

Maat's voice spoke to me as the figures from the Tree drew closer. "All these feminine embodiments that were created from the Tree of Life have come together to initiate you as the Oracle Soljourner."

"Whoa, what do you mean? What's an oracle?" I asked Maat.

"An oracle is someone who offers advice or a prophecy that comes directly from a divine source. Your dreams can be harnessed to look into the future, which will help us in our fight against the darkness," Maat said.

"Is this the 'special gift' I have?"

"Yes, and it is a unique gift, as only a few of us gods and goddesses have this ability. As it is impossible to know exactly what will happen in the future, this gift of yours is also an enormous responsibility."

I wish I had known this earlier so I could have saved Opa, or even Mom and Dad, I thought to myself.

I stood there amongst the goddesses in a large circle beside the Tree of Life. I looked around and saw so many familiar faces; it was like going back to school. So many of them I had grown up with, but thankfully, Rachelle was not there. Each of them had a flicker of green in their eyes—the same glimmer I saw in my own eyes when I looked in the mirror. There was also a constant hum that surrounded us in this place that I had heard back in the Shoe Chamber before. But here, it was a lot clearer now that we were standing so close to the Tree. I could feel it resonate through my body.

Then, to my left, a bright flash of green light startled me, and Ara-Wadjet appeared. Her arrival signaled each of the goddesses to step out of the circle one-by-one, stand before me, and offer me a small, golden box that they each left at my feet. Ara-Wadjet was first, then Georgia, Alexa, Scarlett, Camille as Liberty, Remi as Aine, Jacquie as Ungnyeo, and many more goddesses I had yet to meet, but each one looked like a friend from home.

As the last goddess, Edisia (who looked like my old friend, Franny), came to deliver her box and return to the circle, all of the goddesses joined hands. The boxes at my feet began to glow. They had created a familiar pattern: a spiral.

I looked at Maat and asked, "What are all these boxes?"

Maat turned to me and said, "Orabella, these boxes are gifts. They are precious gems that are connected to each of these goddesses. As you train with each one for your missions, the powers you are taught are amplified by the stone that is given to you. They are called Soul Stones."

I looked down at the boxes, wishing I could open them to see the stones themselves.

Maat spoke again, "These gifts are also for your transition in life."

"What do you mean, Maat? Like becoming a Soljourner or an oracle?"

"No, Orabella. You have also transitioned from being a child to a woman, as you have now begun your Moon Time."

"I haven't felt it yet."

"It is the start of your cycle, Orabella." Maat let a knowing smile touch the corner of her lips.

I blushed. I hadn't felt anything but small stomach cramps—

Oh no, is that what it was?

"Orabella, your Moon Time is an initiation that is natural across all dimensions. We are here to celebrate the birth of your womanhood. You have the power within you to give birth to life, which is the most powerful force in the universe, and your Moon Time is a monthly honouring of that power."

At that moment, the clasped hands of the goddesses began to glow. I felt weird and self-conscious that these powerful women knew something so personal and intimate about me. A lot of my friends back home had already gotten their periods. They mostly complained about how cranky they were and how painful the cramps were. There was no celebration or rejoicing. That weird feeling made me sad that I should immediately feel embarrassed about my Moon Time. Instead, all girls should have experienced this sort of celebration and honour.

At that moment, with the power of the goddesses lighting up around me, I could feel the transformation into womanhood. The light within their hands shot out and hit me. I felt their strength embolden me, and I started to cry and laugh at the same time. I felt a fantastic joy inside of me.

The glowing subsided, and Maat's voice calmed the excitement that had grown inside me. "Orabella, you are not a child anymore, and with that, you are to step into your power and help bring balance back into the universe.

"Not only on Earth, but throughout many realities, the feminine energy has been pushed into submission and not treated equally. There are dark forces in the universe that have not wanted to give form or life to the feminine since the downfall of Atlantis. The goddess concept has been eroded slowly by forces that have poisoned the minds and hearts of humans. But now is the time to fight this imbalance and bring honour back to the creative and powerful process of the feminine."

"Maybe it's Horus," I said.

"Perhaps, Orabella. I have a feeling that Horus is somehow a part of it all. Something has changed. The darkness is spreading." As she said these words, Maat's voice became deep and ominous. Its foreboding tone hung in the air.

I punctuated the sound by asking, "Is that why there are so many goddesses here?"

"We are here to help you, to share our powers and knowledge with you." Her voice had brightened as she answered me.

I paused for a moment. "Maat, I'm excited but also scared."

"Those are normal feelings for your kind, and it is something that could help you along the way. You are not alone. We are all here for each other. If we do not support each other, the feminine energy will die, and eventually, so will the Tree of Life." Maat looked around to each goddess as she said this. Then, she continued. "So, Orabella, please put on the amulet and stand close to the Tree. We are going to create an energy vortex so you will have a direct line with all of us and to the Tree."

"Will this give me more powers?"

"Not exactly. It will allow you to feel how the Tree of Life is faring—whether it is thriving or struggling. It will also allow you to call out to any of us at any time."

The Tree of Life began to glow brighter, and below it, the upside-down Tree of Knowledge did the same. The universal water below us, the goddesses—it all began to hum. It sounded like an "*Ohm.*" I felt a love I had never felt before, and it seemed to wash away all my anger, sadness, and grief.

The golden spiral at my feet intensified in brightness. I knew it was time to walk its curving pathways. My heart was pounding as I put one foot in front of the other. I broke out laughing, feeling so much joy in me. The opened path of the golden box led me to face the Tree of Life. Without touching the Tree, I could still feel a new connection with it. A responsibility. A new awareness. I wiped away the tears that ran down my cheeks, and I knew that my initiation was complete. I turned back to face the goddesses, and one-by-one they unlocked hands and began to fade away from the centre of the universe back to their dimensions.

"Orabella, we are done for now. The Soul Stones will be stored in your Shoe Chamber next to the Emerald Book. I will see you soon in Dreamtime."

I suddenly remembered Oma had put little rivets in the lining of my superhero costume and I had to ask. "Maat, my Oma made me a costume to wear! Could I sew these stones into the fabric?"

"That is an excellent idea, little one. It is indeed."

I smiled as I looked at Maat, but then a shadow behind Maat's shoulder stirred, and my face dropped. I recognized the figure as Theom, the skeleton boy from the Summer Solstice Festival. *How did he get to the centre of the universe? That could not possibly be the real Theom.*

Before I could warn Maat, I was back in the kitchen. I felt dizzy and could hear Lolo meowing. She was back to her normal tabby self, looking up at me with her blue eyes.

I heard footsteps walking towards me, and then my Oma's voice asked, "Orabella, are you okay?"

I looked up at her. "Yes, why?" I asked curiously.

"Your eyes are glowing green and you've been gone for a few minutes. Where is Maat?"

"Really? It felt a lot longer than that. I'm so thirsty." I licked my dry lips.

"I'll get you a glass of water. Please tell me what happened," Oma said, still looking at me with concern.

I recounted the whole experience for her, and then I asked, "Oma, do you remember the first time you got your Moon Time?"

"We didn't call it Moon Time back then. My friends and I were embarrassed to say anything, and we sure didn't talk about it," Oma said, blushing.

"Why, Oma? My mom tells me what to expect, and there was even a class about it in school."

"Exactly, Bella. Back when I was growing up, nobody talked about it. There was shame attached to it, for whatever silly reason."

"I'm sorry, Oma."

Oma and I hugged while Lolo meowed at my feet. I bent down, picked her up, and squeezed her hard against my chest. Growing up could be so confusing and scary at times, but it helped to have people around who loved me.

Suddenly, I bent over. My belly was cramping.

"Bella? Everything okay?" Oma asked.

"Yes, but my stomach hurts."

"Let's get you a hot water bottle to help with the cramps."

"Okay, Oma, thank you."

"Oh, not a problem. We'll have to run into town first thing in the morning to get you some things. Now, up to bed while I get the hot water bottle ready."

As usual, Lolo was already ahead of me and bounded up onto the bed before I could even pull back the blankets. Oma came in a few minutes later with the hot water bottle in hand.

"This will help with your cramps." She placed the flannel-covered rubber bottle on my belly, and I instantly felt better.

"Thank you, Oma."

"Are you hungry?"

"Not really, but thank you."

"Okay, you rest. I'll just be downstairs."

"Oma, thank you. I love you."

"Oh, Bella, I love you too."

Oma left my bedroom. I was content with the hot water bottle on my belly and Lolo next to me, but I saw the tree branches moving outside the window and started thinking about Theom. Who was he? What did he want? *Ouch, another cramp.* I decided to stop thinking about him and call it a day. Then I thought, *I must ask Oma if she can sew the Soul Stones into my costume. Hmm, should I call it the Goddess Oracle Soljourner Costume?* As I brainstormed names, I gradually felt myself drift into Dreamtime.

23

SKELETON BOY—JULY 11TH, 6:30 AM

I woke up, rolled over, and looked at my cell phone. It was so early, but there were more texts from my girls. Then, I checked my calendar. *It's Oma's birthday! I totally forgot!* Since the house was dead quiet, I assumed Oma was still asleep, so I decided I would make her breakfast.

Lolo was stretched out at the foot of my bed. The water bottle had cooled off, but no more cramps, thankfully, and the sun was warming up my room. I was trying to remember my lessons from Dreamtime. I remembered working with Maat. She was by the Tree, but the falcon was not there. Maat was showing me hand positions on the amulet.

"Take your left hand and cup the amulet from the bottom, and then your right-hand cups the top. I want you to focus on your breathing and the shoe that you have chosen. Then, move your hand in a clockwise motion," I remembered Maat saying.

I tried it for a little while but got frustrated and gave up. It was so hard and boring to practice time travel without any of the travelling. I sighed loudly and said, "Why do I have to do this?"

"Because you are an Oracle Soljourner. To perform as such, you must learn to wield all the power that the universe has provided you."

I huffed. "But this is boring!"

Maat responded sternly, "Time travel is challenging. If you can focus on this task now, your future missions will be much easier."

"Can't I just use the necklace that Opa used?" I whined.

"That was the tool that he was provided. The amulet is what you have been given. It is a far more powerful tool. It will enable you to do things that your Opa would never have been able to accomplish. It may seem unimportant to practice with it now, but you will need these exercises soon.

"Remember what's at stake here. I hear your ego speaking, but this is much larger than all of us. You must continue to practice."

I exhaled and released my frustration. "I know you're right, but at times, it's just really hard to focus."

"I know it is, but repetition is the key to making things permanent. I want to add another exercise: while you're focused on your hand movements and your breath, start moving your feet around."

"What? How do I do all of these things at the same time?"

"It is like walking meditation."

Oh, great, it just got harder. I started doing a square dance, back and forth, side to side as my hands were moving clockwise. Then, I brought my attention back to my breath. Soon, with all of these components synchronized, I felt lighter. I opened my eyes and saw that the ground was no longer right beneath my feet. I was hovering above it!

"Whoa, this is cool," I said, but I quickly lost my concentration and fell back on the ground clumsily. "Hey, why do I feel pain here?"

"You're still connected to your physical body, so you're still vulnerable. That's why it's important to focus on the task at hand."

"Okay." I got up off the ground and closed my eyes. I felt my feet moving, my hands rotating, and my breath speeding up, but then I heard a *whoosh*, which distracted me. I opened my eyes. "What was that?"

"The wind?" Maat asked.

"Yes, that whooshing sound."

"It's the cosmic breath that is connected to the Tree and delivers life to all of us. This wind is your carrier between times, as time is interwoven with all of life."

"Okay, I understand. I *do* need more practice."

"Yes, but now I must go. Our session is over."

Then, suddenly, I was in bed. No wonder I was so tired. I felt like I had worked out all night, but I knew it was time to get up to make Oma's birthday breakfast.

I texted Auntie: Are you coming over today for Oma's birthday?

I got dressed and headed downstairs. Oma startled me, as she was already sitting at the kitchen table reading.

"Happy birthday, Oma!" I ran over to give her a big hug.

"Oh, thank you, Bella. How are you feeling? Are you hungry?"

"Don't worry about breakfast. It's your birthday! I'll cook. Just keep reading."

"What a sweet gesture, Orabella, thank you," Oma said as she kissed me on the cheek. "How are your cramps this morning?"

"They're gone," I said cheerily as I gently pushed her out of the kitchen.

I heard Oma turn on the radio in the study. I thought of making a giant omelet with green onions, mushrooms, and cheese, with bacon and sourdough bread on the side. *Yum.* For a moment, I thought about my mom's cooking and how much I missed it.

I heard Oma call out, "Auntie Adri is on the ferry. She'll be here in a short while!"

"Okay! Oma's birthday breakfast in fifteen minutes!"

I pulled everything together and put it on a plate. I ran outside to pick some flowers to put in a vase and placed it in the centre of the table.

"Oma, come sit. I'll bring out breakfast!"

"Okay, sweetie."

I brought out the two plates for each of us and put one directly in front of Oma. "Happy birthday, Oma!"

"Oh my, what a splendid job. Thank you so much. Hmm, maybe you should make breakfast more often—this looks great!"

"Well, I may have to do that."

We were quiet for a moment as we both looked over at the empty seat where Opa used to sit. I felt my eyes get teary but didn't want to upset Oma, so I told Oma a pun. "Oma, pickles celebrate their birthday by relishing the moment every year."

Oma laughed. "I've never heard that one."

"Oma, I was working with Maat in Dreamtime last night."

"Oh?"

As I was about to tell her more, Auntie walked in the door with a box the size of a birthday cake. My eyes widened in excitement. *More cake!* I ran over to grab it.

"Hi, Auntie! Can I help with the box?"

"That would be great. Can you put it in the fridge for me?"

I put the box in the fridge and was about to open it for a sneak peek when I heard Oma say, "Hi, Adri. How was the ride over on the ferry?"

"Hi, Audrey. It wasn't busy at all. Orabella, you seem different, maybe a little older. How odd," Auntie said as I walked back to the table.

"Yes, that's what fresh air will do," Oma said and gave me a quick wink.

There was a knock on the door. I jumped up, hoping and praying that it was Mom and Dad, but it was precisely the opposite. It was Theom, whose eyes were pure black. He was wearing the same costume from the Summer Solstice Festival. For a moment, I froze, not sure how to respond.

My heart was pounding. I grabbed hold of the door handle to slam the door on him, but Theom reached out and touched my arm before I could.

I stared at his black eyes in horror as he said, "You are ours, little one."

I felt nauseous, and something shifted within me. Everything started going dark. Suddenly, it was like everything was frozen except for me. I turned around. Oma and Auntie were fading. No, I was the one disappearing. I reached down to my chest, but the amulet wasn't there. I left it back in the Shoe Chamber. I pushed past Theom and tried to run to the workhouse. I felt him right behind me.

I heard a memory of Opa saying, "Ground yourself!"

I ran to the Tree and stood underneath it. I planted myself like I was a part of the Tree. I looked at Theom in his skeleton costume. I reminded myself that I had made a promise to never give up on myself and that I was in charge of my life.

I stood there and yelled at him, "Who are you?"

Theom laughed. "I am Iblis!"

"I'm ready for you. Bring your worst, because you won't change me. I'm not afraid of you anymore! I won't cheat myself by being afraid anymore. If anything, I want to thank you because you have taught me to appreciate life. To value every second, to love and embrace who I am and what I have become."

I felt the energy of the Tree from behind me, helping me feel connected to the Earth.

"I'm my hero; I'm Orabella, the Oracle Soljourner!" I shouted.

The wind blew stronger, pushing against me. I could feel the Tree holding me in place; I could feel myself getting stronger.

I said aloud, "Challenges in life are meant to make us stronger and not meant to change who we are. If anything, it's to enhance the beauty we already have, so nobody is going to take away who I am!"

The wind stopped and the air grew heavy. I knew what was coming. Suddenly, it got cold, much like what happened at the Community Centre, but it was a different kind of cold. This one was bone-chilling. I stood closer to the Tree. I was not afraid, as I did not permit the darkness to change who I was. The skeleton boy continued to laugh at me.

"Iblis, you have no power over me. I have no fear of you. You almost got me once, but I've become stronger, thanks to you!"

I felt his presence around me. My skin felt sticky.

"Iblis, I'm in control, and you have no power here in this dimension," I told him.

"That's about to change, little one. It is so easy to feed and control humans who are filled with fear and anger, like Rachelle."

"Iblis, you can't scare me or trick me with lies and deceit," I said.

"The darkness is coming, little one. It's beyond anything you could ever imagine," Iblis taunted.

"Iblis, I'm not alone. I have the goddesses behind me, and the light will always outshine the darkness. I have held my own with you all by myself. Imagine what I could do to you when I put on the amulet!"

Iblis let out a roar of laughter.

Above me, on a branch, I heard a twig snap. I looked up and saw a raven looking down at me, holding the amulet in its beak. *Oh no. Morrigan has the amulet!* But to my surprise, she opened her beak and dropped it. I quickly held out my hands to catch it. As soon as it touched my skin, I felt the amulet vibrate. I took it and locked it onto my chest. I was working hard on focusing and grounding the energy within me to make me a conduit, just like the Tree. I felt both the power of the amulet and the presence of the Tree behind me.

Everything started to turn green. Suddenly, a burst of dark energy from Iblis tried to rip the amulet from my chest. I tried to pull away, but I felt it separating me from the amulet. My chest was burning. *Wait, don't resist! Breathe!* Suddenly, a huge green light enveloped me, and a loud shockwave disintegrated the dark energy, knocking Iblis down. He slowly rose and pushed his hands forward. Another burst of dark energy headed my way.

The dark energy bounced off the green force field around me. Morrigan, in her raven form, clawed at Iblis's head and flew away. Lolo jumped onto him, tore at him, and bounced off. Iblis shrieked at the animals, which gave me time to focus on the amulet on my chest. A massive burst of energy blasted out of it, which pushed me back, hard, against the Tree. I ricocheted off the Tree and fell forward onto the ground. I looked up to protect myself, but Iblis and Morrigan were gone.

My body was shaking. I could feel the energy ripple through me. For the first time, I felt that I was one with the amulet. I slowly got up off the ground and raised my fist in triumph.

Wow, did Morrigan try to help me? Then, I realized that—until I felt the power within myself—I would conflict with the amulet's ability.

I stood against the Tree, the power buzzing through me, and I felt at peace with myself. I accepted my mission in life. I felt Lolo push up against me, purring. *Ah yes, my little friend, my constant companion, my superhero sidekick.* "Thank you, Lolo, for your help."

I heard Oma's voice call out, "Orabella, where are you?"

I ran back into the house. Everything seemed to be back to normal.

"Oma, I'm okay. We're all okay."

"What's wrong with your eyes? They're green. How is that possible?" Auntie asked as she pointed her finger at me.

I pulled out the amulet, which was glowing green.

"It's the same colour as your eyes! What just happened?" Auntie asked again.

"Auntie, this is my destiny. To protect the people I love, and to protect the Tree of Life," I said, smiling.

"So, what happened, Orabella?" Oma asked.

"Well, Iblis showed up. I went outside and stood by the Baobab and faced him."

"Are you hurt? Are you okay?" Oma asked with concern.

"I'm good. It is something I felt coming, and I was ready to fight it."

"I'm so proud of you, Orabella. I know it hasn't been easy," Oma said.

"Thanks, Oma. It hasn't, but I'm happy to be here with you," I told her with a soft smile.

"Orabella, no matter how many times your mom tells me about this whole Soljourner thing, it still blows me away," Auntie said, shaking her head.

Then, behind Auntie, Maat and Wadjet appeared, which caught Oma and Auntie by surprise.

"Who are you?" Auntie asked with wide eyes.

"Auntie, this is Maat and Wadjet, the Goddesses who are helping me . . . helping *us*," I said.

"Okay, I knew that gods helped Marcus, Jasper, and the other Soljourners, but wow, I'm meeting a real-life Egyptian goddess."

"Welcome, Adri. It's a pleasure to meet you," Wadjet said.

I wasn't sure if Auntie was about to scream or faint, but Oma grabbed her hand and pulled her off to the side.

"We are very proud of what you did today," Wadjet said.

"Did you know that Iblis would show up?"

"Yes, we did, and we were close by to assist you, but we needed to know how you would react and use your powers."

"So . . . did I pass?"

"Yes, but you need to continue to train. I suggest that Audrey start your homeschooling."

"Yes, Opa mentioned once that my first mission would be to go back to where it all began."

"You listen very well, child. But this is for a far different reason, which goes beyond your mission. We need your help finding out what Horus is up to," Maat said with her kind voice.

"But what about Iblis and the darkness? What about Mom and Dad? How do we get them back?"

"Iblis and the darkness will come, but you require missions to build up your skills to face them. This first trip is more to investigate Horus. As for your father, he's with Horus back in Ancient Egypt," Wadjet said.

"And Mom? Where is she?"

Oma and Auntie suddenly looked surprised, and I felt somebody behind me. I turned to look.

24

SURPRISE RETURN—JULY 11TH, 11:55 AM

"Mom!"

We ran to each other and nearly drowned in a cacophony of warm embraces. Mom gave me a big kiss after big kiss on both cheeks.

"I'm so happy to see you," she said, weeping.

Auntie and Oma ran forward and grabbed hold of us both. Oma grabbed Mom's face and started to cry. "You're back . . . you're okay . . ."

I fell slack against the three of them, utterly relieved that my mom was finally home. After a minute, my mom untangled herself from our hug. She looked to me, her brown eyes grim. "I'm sorry, Orabella, I don't have time to explain, but your father is in trouble, and only you can help him. We must leave now."

Before I could say anything, Auntie protested immediately, "Mary, what do you mean? You just got here! Where have you been?"

Mom didn't respond to Auntie, so Auntie spoke up again, "You can't leave just like that! What happened to you?"

"From what I could gather," Mom started breathlessly, "Horus tried to erase me from time, but it was a trick to get Marcus to help him with something. I was hiding in the Void until Maat found me and brought me here. I wasn't there for very long—maybe only a few minutes."

I turned to look for Maat, but she had disappeared, and so had Wadjet. I turned back when my aunt cried hysterically, "Well, for us, that was twelve days ago! Today is July 11th!"

"Oh, my! It feels like I just left the bedroom . . . wait a minute! It's your birthday today, Audrey," Mom said, putting a hand on Oma's shoulder, then she looked at me with tears in her eyes, "I'm sorry I missed your birthday, Bella!"

I looked at my mom with admiration that she could think of others at a time like this—she was always so generous.

Auntie spoke again as she threw her arms back around her sister. "Sis, I missed you. I don't understand what's going on, but I love you so much."

"Thank you, Adri. I was so scared without any of you," my mom said as she hugged her back tightly.

I found it cute to watch them wipe the tears off their cheeks in the same way.

Suddenly, something hit me—the dream I had about the shadow in the corner and the feeling it was going to betray me . . . us . . . I was being warned that it was Horus. *Why was I being told it was Horus if, in my gut, he didn't seem like the culprit of all our wrongdoing? I had to find out who was the cause of all of this trouble.*

"Please bring my son back safely." Oma's pleading brought me back to the present.

"I will, Audrey, I promise. Maat told me that Orabella is the one who will bring Marcus back because of her special gift." Mom paused for a long moment and then looked around the room. "Where's Jasper?" she asked.

We all looked at each other, not sure who would tell Mom, but Oma spoke up. "I'm sorry to tell you, Mary, but Jasper passed away just recently. It was a car accident." Oma teared up all over again.

Mom was shocked. "I'm so sorry to hear that; he was so special." She pulled Oma into a hug.

Lolo came into the kitchen, meowing, and went right to Mom, who picked her up. "So good to see you, Lolo. I'm sure you have taken good care of Orabella."

Lolo meowed, and Mom passed her on to me. I gave her a big squeeze.

"Could we take Lolo with us, Mom?"

"Yes, Orabella, of course. She's your protector. Maat says that we needed to go back to the exact time when the Soljourners began. That's where your father is."

"Yes, Maat told us that before you arrived."

"Oh, is she here?" Mom asked.

"Yes, she and another goddess named Wadjet popped in together. Scared the daylights out of me. I've only heard about all these stories, but to experience it firsthand has been very scary," Auntie said.

"I'm sure it has been, sis."

"Orabella, do you have your amulet with you?" Oma asked.

In response to her question, I took the amulet out of my pocket and locked it onto my chest. It clung there, and I felt its energy run through me. I closed my eyes and focused on my breathing.

I felt the ripple of energy getting stronger, and the ringing in my ears began. For the first time, I saw the Tree of Life in front of me. I saw a direct line of energy from the Tree to the amulet and from the amulet to me. I saw a pulse of energy running through the Tree-like it was breathing. Its pulse went into me, and I felt my body warming up. I opened my eyes and saw that everything was green. Oma, Auntie, and Mom were looking back at me in shock.

I looked down and saw green energy all around me. I felt it and knew the power was building in my hands.

"Orabella, what's going on?" Mom asked.

"Mary, it's the amulet. It's connected to the Book, and she is connected to both," Oma told her.

"Okay, this is pretty weird," Auntie Adri said as she backed away from me. She looked like she was getting ready to run out of the house.

"I'm okay, everybody," I said in response to the concerned looks on their faces.

"But you're glowing green, and your eyes are green, too," Mom exclaimed.

I looked down at my hands and couldn't help but think that I should write a book about this or maybe even better, a comic book that I could call *Oracle of Shoes.*

"Orabella, are you daydreaming again?" Oma broke me out of my thoughts.

"Sort of," I said sheepishly.

Mom continued staring at me while she said, "Well, it seems like a lot has happened while I was away. I can't believe Jasper is gone."

"Also, Mom, I got my Moon Time," I said enthusiastically. I unlocked the amulet from my chest, watching the green around me fade away and the energy subside.

Mom started to cry even more. "I was only gone for a moment, but I missed a lifetime of experiences. So much has happened. I'm sorry I wasn't there!"

"Oh, Mary, it's not your fault. You did what you had to do," Oma said.

"The last thing I remember from the house was Marcus telling you to call Opa. It broke my heart to see how scared you were and how there was nothing I could do."

"It's okay, Mom," I said as I hugged her close to me.

Maat appeared in the kitchen again. "It is time for us to go."

"Olivia?" Mom asked.

"Mom, this is not Olivia. It's Maat."

"This is not the Maat I met in the Void."

"I'm sorry," said Maat. "I appeared to you in my original form. It's only in this dimension that I have to switch to a form that you recognize immediately."

Auntie looked like a deer in headlights, trying to figure it all out.

It was at that moment that I thought about all that had happened in the last two weeks—how my life had changed forever. I felt happy to have my mom back, but I was simultaneously sad and confused for having to go back in time to save my dad and to face Horus, the creator of the Soljourners. I grabbed Mom, who had massive tears in her eyes, and I looked back at Oma and Auntie, who both looked sad. I wondered if I would ever see them again. I looked towards Maat.

"Wait, I just realized something. In one of my dreams within a dream, I was reading this newspaper article where this person was looking for somebody to go time travelling with him. The P.O. box is 0427."

"That's Marcus's birthday," Mom said.

"I just figured it out, but I think Dad was trying to send a message to me through the dream. It also said you would get paid after we got back and that you must bring your own weapon. He also wrote that he had to do what he did several times and needed to save a friend. What do you think, Maat?" I asked.

"It sounds like a riddle or a warning," Maat said.

"Okay, but I think Dad left something in that mailbox at 2949 Main Street. Maybe at some point in the past, he put something in it," I said.

"Well, it is possible. Maybe Marcus was warning us of a trap that we could be heading into," Oma replied.

"Good point. I think it's worth checking out," Mom said.

Before I could even blink, Maat, Mom, and I arrived at the post office. A clerk came out from the back.

"Hello. Can I help you?"

Mom replied, "Yes, we're looking for mailbox number 0427. Unfortunately, we lost our key."

"Oh, do you have I.D. to verify the account?"

Mom looked down at her nightgown before responding, "Oh, I'm sorry. I left my wallet at home."

The clerk froze.

"We cannot wait any longer," Maat said impatiently. She turned her hand, and one of the boxes opened. I went up to it and, sure enough, it was the right one. I looked inside and couldn't believe my eyes. It was the same key that was in my dream, the one with the spiral at the top and the green gem in the middle. I also noticed a journal in the mailbox. *Is it the same journal in the picture with Dad?* I took the key from the box and turned to Mom and Maat, holding the key in the open palm of my hand and leaving the journal in the mailbox. I stood between the mailbox and Mom and Maat so they did not notice the journal.

"Do you know what this key is for?" Mom asked.

"I think it's a clue to something that Dad left for us to find."

Before Mom could respond, Maat grabbed our hands. With my spare hand, I stretched out to grab the journal from the mailbox, hoping Mom and Maat did not notice. I shoved it down my pants. Then, the loud *whoosh* of time travel overtook us.

I landed hard on the ground on my hands and knees. There was sand everywhere, even in my mouth, which I spat out. Mom was close by, standing up and brushing sand off of her nightgown. I looked around me but didn't see Maat anywhere. There was a massive wall behind us, like we were standing outside of a city. Sand continued to blow around us and the sun blazed down upon us.

"I have a feeling we're in Ancient Egypt. *Really* Ancient Egypt," Mom said.

"Why do you say that?"

"Well, the Great Pyramids haven't been completed yet," she said as she pointed out over the horizon towards the half-built pyramids.

"Oh," I said, my eyes following her pointed finger.

Mom was silent. I turned and saw her staring at something in the distance with shock on her face.

"How is this possible? What are you doing here?" she exclaimed.

I looked to where she was staring and saw a young woman standing there. Something about her was eerily familiar. *Hold on. This cannot be happening. Has a future's past event been created?* Mom just stood there in disbelief, as if she had seen a ghost. I checked my pocket and realized that I didn't have the amulet with me.

"Wait, I just realized something," I said, calling out to the woman who had just materialized. "You're the spy I have been warned about! How could you?"

I suddenly felt a hand on my shoulder, and a familiar voice whispered into my ear, "Gotcha!"

AFTERWORD

Who is this young woman that Orabella and her mom recognize? Who is the spy that Orabella was warned about? Who grabbed Orabella's shoulder? Will Orabella be able to rescue her dad? What happened to the amulet and Maat? Is Maat an enemy working with Horus or Iblis? What is Oma's secret that has yet to be revealed? Who are the allies, and who are the enemies?

Thank you for reading
Then and There, Here and Where.

Please consider posting a rating or review to sites like Goodreads and Amazon.

Reviews are the lifeblood of authors and help more readers like you find their new favourite books!

ACKNOWLEDGEMENTS

We would like to thank my Oma Audrey and Grandpa Randy, who have given so much to our family; my sister, Lauren, my brother, Lucas, Opa and Nona, and the rest of our family and friends who have supported us through our goals. Also the real Global Girls Squad, who have supported us along our journey.

You make us stronger by believing in us and believing in the vision we have created. We are thankful to Sylvia Taylor, Genevieve Zander and GenZ Publishing for the hours upon hours of editing. Morissa Schwartz for believing in us. We would also like to thank Variety BC and *KGMS* for their work with kids with learning challenges. And for everybody who has a learning challenge, believe in yourself. You're not alone. Build confidence in your strengths.

ABOUT ESABELLA STRICKLAND

Esabella (Bella) Strickland, daughter of Michael and Kate, is the real inspiration behind the Orabella the Oracle journeys. An award-winning actress, multi award-winning filmmaker and writer, artist, media host, and Gen Z influencer, Esabella is a voice for children with learning disabilities as a Variety BC Ambassador. Her motto is, "Lift as you rise."

Visit her online:

www.esabellakarena.com

ABOUT MICHAEL STRICKLAND

Michael Strickland's passion for bringing wellness to the world stems from over two decades in the healing arts. Along with learning a variety of healing modalities, Michael apprenticed with a shaman, Misha Ma, in Mongolia. As a healer and a father, his insight comes from the countless stories he has listened to over many years. It is Michael's passion that this new storytelling project is brought to life through writing.

Visit him online:

www.michaelstricklandproductions.com

Made in the USA
Monee, IL
05 April 2021

64764723R00152